He shouldn't be here

This woman was beautiful. This woman was intelligent and funny. This woman was eccentric. This woman was engaged to another man.

He should get out of here—right now. But his daughter had come alive. Maddy had been with him for three months now and she'd been flat and listless and disinterested the whole time.

And Bryony had made her laugh. You could forgive a lot in a woman who made your daughter laugh.

Trisha David is a country girl, born on a southeast Australian dairy farm. She moved on—mostly because the cows just weren't interested in her stories! Married to a "very special doctor," Trisha writes medical romances as Marion Lennox and Harlequin Romance® books as Trisha David. In her other life she cares for kids, cats, dogs, chickens and goldfish. She travels, she fights her rampant garden (she's losing) and her house dust (she's lost!)— oh, and she teaches statistics and computing to undergraduates at her local university.

Books by Trisha David

HARLEQUIN ROMANCE
3472—McALLISTER'S BABY
3494—McTAVISH AND TWINS

Don't miss any of our special offers. Write to us at the following address for information on our newest releases.

Harlequin Reader Service
U.S.: 3010 Walden Ave., P.O. Box 1325, Buffalo, NY 14269
Canadian: P.O. Box 609, Fort Erie, Ont. L2A 5X3

Falling for Jack
Trisha David

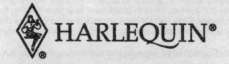

HARLEQUIN®

TORONTO • NEW YORK • LONDON
AMSTERDAM • PARIS • SYDNEY • HAMBURG
STOCKHOLM • ATHENS • TOKYO • MILAN • MADRID
PRAGUE • WARSAW • BUDAPEST • AUCKLAND

ISBN 0-373-03558-6

FALLING FOR JACK

First North American Publication 1999.

Copyright © 1998 by Trisha David.

Printed in U.S.A.

CHAPTER ONE

JACK MORGAN was a farmer who had spent six years trying to remove emotion from his life.

He had failed. Maddy was watching from the ringside, and the love he felt for her was almost overwhelming. And in the ring there was Jessica—and who wouldn't fall for Jessica?

It had to end. Perfection couldn't continue for ever. There was a lump rising in Jack's throat as he prepared to give the last command.

The sheep were bunched neatly outside the final gate. Jack lifted his fingers to his mouth and gave a piercing whistle. It didn't have the effect Jack intended.

A small grey dog raced from under the stands. This wasn't a sheepdog like Jessica. This dog was squat and stocky, with white tufts on his chest, bristly black eyebrows and a wiry grey moustache and beard. The dog galumphed rather than raced, his pudding frame pounding up a dust storm. He yapped. Jack gave another frantic whistle.

'Get them in, Jess. Now! One more minute and you'll have them penned and be Australian champion.'

Jess wouldn't be Australian champion. The strange dog launched himself straight into the mob. Sheep sprayed outward as if a bomb were exploding, and there was nothing Jessica or Jack or any power on earth could do to stop them. The sheep headed for the fence. The mutt headed after them—and Jessica followed. Jack stood alone in the ring. Stunned.

'*Harry!*' A woman was calling frantically from somewhere in the crowd.

Jack couldn't see who was yelling. All he could see was

chaos. For a bunch of farmers, what was happening was crazy. People parted to make way for escaping sheep. No one moved to stop them. The first sheep to hit the fence ducked under the bar. Then the mutt raised his yap rate and the last few took the fence as a hurdle.

The fence wasn't designed to keep sheep in. This was a trialling ground for sheepdogs, and sheepdogs knew their stuff. Young or badly trained dogs mightn't control a mob as they ought, but the most ill-trained dog could at least hold them together.

But not now. Even if Jessica was still interested in sheepdog work—which she wasn't—the sheep had scattered too widely to stop them.

Bryony Lester stared around her with dismay. To put it mildly, this was terrible! Myrna had told Bryony that to bring Harry to the show was a great way to introduce herself to the locals. Well, the locals would know her now. They'd probably tar and feather her and run her out of town.

'Good one, Myrna!'

As Bryony muttered invective to her absent friend, a fat and frantic sheep thumped into her legs, veered sideways, and headed for the horizon.

'I'll kill you, Harry,' Bryony said out loud. 'Mutton's off the menu and schnauzer's on!' She cupped her hands and yelled again for her stupid dog, but she just knew it wasn't going to work.

Spectators were scattering in all directions. Some were making a token effort to catch sheep, but others simply stared open-mouthed, stunned that, for the first time in years, Jack Morgan had missed out on first prize. The dogs disappeared completely before Jack Morgan recovered enough to yell for his dog to return.

'*Jessica!*'

Jack's best sheepdog-training voice boomed out over the general chaos. Nothing happened. No black and white dog appeared from the crowd. No Jessica.

What appeared was a woman. Bryony. And Bryony Lester was *some* woman!

Bryony was tall and willow slim. She had on white leggings and boots and a vast cream sweater that almost reached her knees. The only colour about her was her huge green eyes and a blaze of red curls tumbling to her shoulders.

Oh, and maybe her cheeks. Her face was chagrin-pink, turning fast to mortification-scarlet!

'Oh, help... Harry, where on earth...?'

Bryony stopped mid-sentence as she came face to face with Jack. And Jack knew... Jack just knew that this woman and disaster walked hand in hand. She was behind this. She had to be. The absent Harry she was calling and the sheep-chasing mutt must be one and the same.

So Jack stepped over the fence—no problem for the departing sheep and even less for the six-foot-two-inch Jack—and he met her head-on.

'Is that mutt yours?'

Jack's voice—raised a minute ago to yell for Jessica—now lowered to whisper-quiet, but his clipped words carried.

'Harry's a small grey dog?' he demanded as Bryony failed to answer. His solid frame blocked her path.

Bryony stopped short. Oh, heck... This man had been in the ring with the sheepdog. She'd seen him. In fact, maybe it was because she'd been too intent on looking at him— well, who wouldn't look at a man like this?—that Harry had been able to wriggle free.

A man had no business to be as good-looking as this.

'I'm... Yes, that's Harry.' Bryony took three deep breaths and fought for calm. The farmer was standing right before her, his muscled frame blocking everything else.

Making it hard for her to think of anything else! 'Were they…are they your sheep?'

'They're not my sheep,' Jack told her. His one-syllable words were spoken slowly so even the stupid could understand, and he was glaring as if she were some faintly repellent insect. 'They're owned by the agricultural committee. They're here for the dog trials.'

Bryony looked wildly around.

'Oh, no… And now they've gone. And they'll take ages to round up.'

Faint grinding of teeth.

'I imagine they will.'

Jack's voice was now so low, Jack's dogs would have recognised danger and headed straight under the shearing shed. And stayed there.

Bryony gulped. This man wasn't helping her mortification level one bit. She tried again. 'I'm so sorry. Can you…? Could you please tell me where to go, then?'

Jack thought of all the places he'd like to tell her to go. His manners won the day, but only just.

'What for?'

Bryony stared at her boots for a long moment—and then tilted her chin and looked at him, face to face.

Bryony Lester did have courage.

'To apologise.'

Silence.

From all around, there were yells and whoops as the local kids launched themselves at sheep. The sounds suggested the sheep were winning, no sweat. But the man and woman stood staring at each other. In silence.

It went on and on.

In another situation this pair could have been classed as a lovely couple. Bryony was five feet eight or so. Jack was about six inches taller and a few years older. Jack looked mid-thirties. In fact, Jack was thirty-four to Bryony's twenty-eight. But… Maybe they looked too much as if they came from different backgrounds to be classed as a couple.

Jack was wind-burned, lithe and muscular, and looked as if he was straight off the land. His cropped black curls held a layer of dust from the showground under his broad-brimmed hat, and his moleskins and open-neck shirt looked as if they'd seen years of hard work. The crinkling of his deep-set eyes, as if they were permanently shielded against a too harsh sun, augmented the impression of a man who worked the land for a living.

In contrast, Bryony looked pretty and flustered, and as if she'd never seen a sheep or a farm in her life.

'If you want to apologise, you might try *me*,' Jack said at last.

'Pardon?' Jack's voice was cutting right through to her now. Bryony didn't need Jessica to tell her that Jack's tone was dangerous. If there'd been a shearing shed handy, she'd have crawled under it herself.

'You might try apologising to *me*.' Jack's strongly boned jaw clamped into a long line of disapproval. 'That mutt—'

'He's not a mutt. He's a schnauzer!'

'What kind of dog is that?'

Bryony's green eyes flashed. Nobody criticised her Harry. 'He's a great dog. Schnauzers are bred in Germany as guard dogs.'

'Then why didn't you leave him in Germany?'

Bryony flushed some more. She ran a hand through her flaming hair, tumbling the curls back from her face. And tried again.

'Look, I did apologise to you, but I'll say it again. I'm really sorry, Mr...?'

She stopped and waited, expectant.

'Morgan,' Jack said grudgingly. 'Jack Morgan.'

'And I'm Bryony Lester.' Bryony held out a slim hand and smiled up at him—a smile that in days past might have knocked the stuffing right out of Jack. It was an absolutely stunning smile.

But, for Jack Morgan, women's smiles were a thing of the past.

'Yeah, right.' He looked down at Bryony's hand, and chose to ignore it. 'Get your dog back,' he said flatly.

Bryony's smile faded, and her hand dropped. She stared up at the man before her and saw nothing but anger in his face.

Which was a shame. The creases around the man's eyes looked as if they should be laughter lines. His face was open and honest. A man like this—a man as good-looking as he was and with a dog like his—ought to be smiling for the sheer pleasure of being alive.

Especially here, Bryony thought. The showgrounds were set in the lee of the Garriwerd mountain range. Bryony had been told this was the best grazing country in all of Southern Australia, and she could believe it. Rich, undulating pastures were dotted with vast river red gums. It was spring and the sun had enough warmth to soothe and caress. The showgrounds were set by a river that was as broad as it was beautiful.

All in all, it was a setting and a season to make you glad to be alive. Unless you were this man.

This man wasn't going to smile. No way.

'I don't know whether I can get Harry back,' Bryony confessed doubtfully. 'I think he's fallen for your dog—and he's not very obedient.'

'I can see that.'

'Can you make your dog come? Harry might come with her.'

It was a forlorn hope. There were so many fantastic smells in this place. Hot dogs. Doughnuts. Cow dung...

Jack didn't answer. Instead he put a finger to each side of his mouth and whistled—and Bryony jumped about a foot. Jack's whistle could have woken the dead two states away. And ten seconds later Jessica slunk through the legs of the crowd and sidled apologetically back to her master.

Bryony was just plain astounded. With the smells of hot dogs, cows and all, Jessie had come back. No matter how Bryony whistled, Harry never came for her.

Then she stared down in concern as the black and white collie pressed herself close to Jack's leg. The collie clearly knew that she'd messed things up. Her tail was tucked between her legs, her ears were flattened and her huge brown eyes looked beseechingly up at Jack in abject apology.

And Bryony knew exactly what her disreputable Harry had seen in her.

'Oh, you darling…' Bryony gave a delighted chuckle and sank down onto the dust—white leggings and all. 'You're gorgeous. Don't look like that. It wasn't your fault. Your Jack's not going to blame you. Not when it was Harry's fault…'

'Don't touch my dog.'

Jack's voice was a growl and Bryony looked up in amazement.

'Why on earth not?'

'She's been taught not to let strangers touch her.'

'Don't be ridiculous. She knows I won't hurt her.' And Bryony put her arms around Jess and gave her a hug.

The dog's ears lifted. Jessica stopped looking up at Jack, and her tail gave a tiny, questioning wag. And then a stronger one. This was okay, her tail said. Jessie nuzzled into Bryony's cream sweater, decided she liked the sensation very much, and gave Bryony a long, loving kiss from neck to eyebrows.

So much for Jack's training that she should growl and withdraw if anyone but family touched her. Jack stared down in stunned amazement. And, to his horror, he felt a totally stupid surge of something that felt very like jealousy.

Jealousy for a dog? He caught himself sharply and tried once more.

'Will you leave my dog alone?'

Bryony chuckled again—a soft, melodic sound that rang out over the trial ground as a sound of happiness. Irrationally, it set Jack's teeth on edge. Luckily, this time Bryony obeyed his command. She rose and brushed the dust from her leggings. They were some leggings. Bryony's legs seemed to go on for ever, and her clinging pants left little to the imagination. She had curves just where a woman ought to have curves...

Cut it out, Jack! Jack caught himself staring, and hauled himself back to anger with an almost visible effort.

'Your dog's still chasing the sheep,' he said harshly. 'Get him back.'

Bryony moistened her lips.

'Like...how?'

'Like I got my dog back. Call him.'

'Well, short of borrowing a bugle, I can't get a sound as loud as yours. And he'll be halfway across the showground by now.' Bryony paused and gave Jack a small, placating smile. 'Actually, even if I'm six feet away Harry doesn't come when I call. Unless I'm eating. Then he does a back flip to get to me.'

'You feed your dog what you eat yourself—?' Jack broke off in disgust. 'Oh, for Pete's sake... Look, just get your dog and clear out of here, Miss...Miss Whatever-your-name-is.'

'I'm Bryony,' she said again, and this time she forced him to take her hand by simply reaching out and grasping his. 'I knew you weren't listening last time.' She took his fingers between hers and shook, regardless. 'Bryony Lester.'

Jack did a mental back flip. Bryony's hand was firm yet soft, and she smelled of something fragrant... Something really good.

'Bryony...' Jack said her name automatically—as if he was saying it despite himself.

'I'll go and find Harry,' Bryony said apologetically, disengaging her fingers. 'I guess he'll have sheep up trees by now. But don't worry, Mr Morgan. He won't hurt them. He brought me one of Myrna's ducklings last week and when he put it down the little thing waddled straight back to its mother. Wasn't that clever of him to be so gentle?'

'*Brilliant.*' Jack had recovered a smidgen of his equilibrium—and his bad temper. His voice said Harry was anything but brilliant.

Bryony sighed and turned away. Hopeless. This man was so good-looking he could make her toes curl, but hopeless!

'Jack!'

A shout from the sidelines made her hesitate. A middle-aged man in a suit—incongruous in a land of denim jeans and moleskins—was heading straight for them. A large badge proclaimed him: *Brian McKenzie. Judge—Working Dog Trials.* He looked brimful of self-importance, and despite the discomfiture Jack Morgan was making her feel Bryony waited to hear what he had to say.

'Jack, I'm sorry, mate, but we've had to disqualify you,' the man told Jack. He directed a lingering look at Bryony and then turned his attention reluctantly back to Jack. 'It's rules,' he said shortly. 'Your dog should be able to cope with distractions.'

Jack's look, stormy before, turned to thunder.

'Another dog launching himself into the mob while Jess works is hardly just a distraction.'

'The rule book doesn't say anything about that,' the man told him. 'We checked. Sorry, mate.'

'Hell…'

'There's always next month,' the man assured him, not meeting his eyes. 'And Tom Higgins will enjoy getting first prize for a change.'

Then the man cast one last appreciative look at Bryony—and headed for his judges' stand before Jack could argue.

'Oh,' Bryony said in a small voice, watching Jack's face. 'That doesn't seem fair.'

'No.' Jack's voice was stretched like fencing wire, almost to breaking point. 'It's not.'

'Do you think if I went and explained…apologised…?'

'It wouldn't make any difference. I can appeal, but it'll be fought every inch of the way and it's just not worth it. That man is Tom Higgins' father-in-law.'

'Tom Higgins... The competitor who'll win now?'

'That's the one.'

'I see.' Bryony looked doubtfully up at Jack. Then her face cleared a little. 'Well, I guess it's not like it's money or anything. Harry and I were watching you and I thought your Jessica was gorgeous. The best. Harry thought so too. That's why he tried to meet her. So you still have the best dog, with or without first prize.'

And then, as Jack's expression still stayed stormy, she tried again. 'Actually, Harry and I didn't win first prize either. In fact, we didn't win any prize. Harry cocked his leg on the judge's lovely shoes. Edna McKenzie. Do you know her? The poor lady nearly had kittens.'

Jack's eyes widened. Edna McKenzie...wife of Brian. It couldn't have happened to a more satisfactory person.

A tiny muscle at the side of Jack's mouth quivered—so slightly that Bryony thought she might have imagined it. His jaw clamped back down straight away, though. Clearly Jack Morgan was intent on nursing his grievance.

'You weren't here for obedience trials?' Jack's voice was frankly incredulous.

'Well, no.' Bryony smiled up at him, refusing to be daunted by his grouchiness. 'We were trying for champion schnauzer. Harry's a pedigree. Myrna said I should show him and maybe someone would pay a stud fee for his services.' She chuckled. 'Harry would love that. At the moment he practises on cushions and on my leg and on anything else he can find. It'd be nice to channel his interest into a more natural direction.'

Once more, there was that almost imperceptible twitch.

This man was really something, Bryony thought. If she could only get him to smile...

And then she paused as a child materialised at Jack's side. The child was about six years old, and she was thin to the point of emaciation. Her fair hair was dragged off her face in two long, uneven pigtails and her denim dungarees hung loose on her body. She looked like an escapee from an Orphan Annie movie.

'Jack, Jessie didn't win.'

A thin, reedy voice. Flat. Intensely disappointed. And, for the first time, Bryony felt a surge of real guilt. It hadn't been too bad up until now. Bryony had reasoned that she hadn't meant to let Harry slip his collar and, even if Jack Morgan had missed out on first prize, it couldn't be so important. This was a small country show and everyone knew Jessica was far and away the best dog.

But this little one had wanted Jess to win. The loss was aching in her voice, and Bryony felt just dreadful, so she dropped to her knees again, her leggings making two cups in the dust. She had supreme disregard for her white leggings.

As well she might, Jack thought. Even coated six inches thick in dust, Bryony's leggings would look wonderful on Bryony.

'I'm afraid that was all my dog's fault,' Bryony confessed to the little girl, oblivious of Jack watching her. 'He chased Jessica's sheep. Did you see him? Harry's a bad dog and I don't know what I'm going to do with him.'

'Jessie won't be Australian champion now.'

The child's voice wasn't accusing. She was just telling the facts.

'How do you mean?' Bryony looked up at Jack. 'I... This is only a small show. I mean, surely it's not like it's the Australian championships or anything.'

'It is,' the child said sadly. 'You get points for every show you win, but you have to get all your points in a year. Jack said Jess only needed one more show and this was it. And we were going to put Jessie's trophy in my room because Jack lets Jessie sleep on my bed...'

She stopped, her huge brown eyes filled with tears, and Bryony felt about two inches tall.

'I'm so sorry.' Bryony's voice fell uselessly away. One look at this little girl told Bryony there was more at stake here than a trophy. The child had every appearance of a waif—a waif who'd wanted a trophy so much it hurt.

'Hey, Maddy, there's one more show. One more show before we run out of time.' Ignoring Bryony, Jack stooped to lift the child into his arms, but the little girl refused to be comforted. She held herself ramrod-stiff, refusing to sink into his hold.

'But it'll be her last chance,' she whispered. 'What if something happens then?' Maddy hardly seemed to be speaking to the man who was holding her. It was a conversation with herself. She was pushing all her distress inward.

'Do you think something like this could happen a second time?' Jack hugged the child and smiled into her troubled eyes, and it was the smile Bryony had expected and more. It was a smile that could turn a heart right over. Gorgeous white teeth flashed out in his weathered face, transforming it to laughter, and his deep brown eyes crinkled as if they were accustomed to smiling. There was humour in Jack's face, and there was kindness and there was sympathy.

There was love for this little one written all over him, and it was a smile to make hearts stand still. Whew! But Maddy held herself aloof.

'If Miss Lester promises to leave her dog at home, we'll win next time,' Jack promised the child. Jack cast a doubtful look across at Bryony. 'And I don't think she'll be here again. She's not local.'

Of course she isn't local, his look said. No one this dumb could be a local.

'Well, I am local,' Bryony said, hauling herself upright again to meet his look with defiance. 'I've just moved here.'

The child stared at her from Jack's arms.

'What's your name?' she asked cautiously.

'Bryony.'

The child considered. 'Bryony's pretty,' she pronounced. 'Mine's Madelaine but my... People call me Maddy.'

'I'm pleased to meet you, Maddy.' Bryony didn't put her

hand out to greet her. There was something about this child that said she wasn't into being touched. Not even by the man who was holding her.

'I've just moved here, too,' the child said. 'Where did you come from?'

'Well, this time I've moved from New York.'

'But...New York's in America.'

'Hey, that's right.' Bryony beamed her approval and Maddy gave her a shy smile.

'My grandma lived in America,' Maddy confided. 'I don't expect you knew her. We lived in California.'

'You're American?' Bryony had already guessed. It was obvious when Maddy spoke. The man was broadly Australian, but the child definitely wasn't. 'Wow. I'm *very* pleased to meet you, Maddy. I spent the last few years in the States and I'm homesick. It was Thanksgiving last week and no one here knew about it but me. I had to eat my turkey all by myself. Are you homesick?'

Maddy cast a doubtful look at Jack.

'Y-yes.'

'Have your family moved here?'

'No.' The child's face clamped down. Her lips pressed together and there was a look of pain in her face that told Bryony to ask that question had been really dumb. The child took a deep breath, as if she was about to confess something shameful. And she did.

'My mom doesn't want me,' she said bleakly. 'My grandma did, but she's dead. I have to live with my father now.'

Oh.

'I see.' Bryony looked doubtfully at Jack, her heart sinking.

Jack. This must be the father, then, in the 'I have to live with my father...' There was definitely a resemblance. The eyes were the same. And the firmness of the set mouth.

'This is your daddy?'

'My mom says Jack's my father.' The child's voice said

she didn't believe a word of such a stupid statement. Maddy
gave an uncompromising wriggle in Jack's arms. 'I want
to get down.' She was set on the ground by a silent Jack,
and she stared up at Bryony with interest. Her father was
discarded. 'Where's your bad dog gone to now?'

'I don't know.' Bryony hesitated. There were things
going on here she didn't understand in the least, but maybe
they weren't her business. 'I guess I'd better go find him.'

Should she, though? What were her priorities here?
Bryony looked dubiously over at the stands. One sheep was
right up at the top of the seating, trying to figure whether
jumping down into the Haunted House was worth the risk.
That was the only sheep in sight. Heaven knew where the
rest were. 'Maybe I'd best help catch the sheep first.'

'At the risk of giving offence, Miss Lester,' Jack told her
dryly, 'you'd be more help just catching your dog. Jessica
and I will round up the sheep. You concentrate on getting
your dog under control.'

'Harry could help find them!'

'And then he'd keep chasing them.' Jack shoved his wide
hat down further over his eyes, forming a barrier of
shadow. 'They'd end up in Queensland. Just find your dog
and keep him out of trouble. That's all I ask.' He held out
his hand to his daughter. 'Come on, Maddy.'

Maddy considered Jack's hand and shook her head,
firmly. Instead, to Bryony's surprise, she reached out and
tucked her hand into Bryony's.

'I'll help Bryony find Harry.'

'Maddy...' Jack's voice took on a tone of exasperation,
and the child froze, and cringed, looking up at Jack as if
she expected to be struck.

'Hell!' Jack swore, and then he knelt so his eyes were
level with the child's. He sighed as the fear in the child's
eyes didn't fade a bit. 'It's okay, Maddy.' His voice softened, but there was defeat in his tone. 'You go hunt for
bad dogs with Miss Lester.' He looked up at Bryony. 'Can
I trust you to bring her back here when you've found him?'

'Of course.' Bryony glared. Jack Morgan might look like an absolute hunk, but there was no denying his temper—or that Maddy was afraid of him. Jack saw the thought, for Bryony didn't attempt to hide it and this man was astute. He flinched.

'I don't hurt her,' he said, and there was pain behind his words. 'I never have and I never would. I promise you. Things aren't what they seem.'

Bryony looked into his eyes—and believed him.

'Yeah, well...'

Who knew what was happening here? Certainly not Bryony. She flicked her hair back from her face and tried for nonchalance. 'We'll leave you to your sheep, then, Mr Morgan,' she managed. 'Let's go find Harry, Maddy Morgan.'

CHAPTER TWO

THEY found Harry fifteen minutes later and Harry was neck-deep in trouble. Or rather he was neck-deep in dung.

The cattle pavilions were the last place they searched. Bryony nosed her way through the cows, Maddy clinging to her side, and there was Harry rolling with canine delight in a pile of fresh manure.

The dog looked up as he saw Bryony. Bryony! Source of dog food, toast and electric blankets. He struggled to his feet, cocked a mucky eyebrow at his mistress, quivered all over from nose to stump—and launched himself at her with love. Straight into her arms. It was the only trick Bryony had been able to teach him—to fly straight up into her arms. He trusted her absolutely to grasp him and not to let him fall as he jumped.

So Bryony had no choice. She grasped as expected and Harry wagged himself all over in her arms. Green dung dripped straight down the front of her cream sweater and further, onto her white leggings.

Bryony stood on the concrete floor of the cattle pavilion, thinking longingly of goldfish as pets and wondering whether schnauzers made good goldfish food.

'He *is* a bad dog!' By her side, Maddy was breathless in horrified awe.

'He certainly is.' Bryony took a deep breath—then decided she didn't need to breathe again for a while. Harry looked adoringly up through his bushy eyebrows and wagged his stump of a tail. It was too much. Around them there was shocked silence as the cattlemen saw what Harry had done, but Bryony's mouth was curving into a grin she couldn't contain. She either laughed here or she sat down amid the dung and howled. So she laughed and, with relief, the cattlemen laughed with her.

'Can I give you a hose down, miss?' one of them asked her—semi-serious—and Bryony thought, Why not? She held her dog before her as the farmer directed his hose full blast. After all, it would serve Harry right and it couldn't make the mess worse. Could it?

It could. The dung had soaked in too far to be rinsed off by a spray with cold water. Now, instead of being almost dry and manured, she was soaking wet and manured. The dung mixed with the water and soaked right in to her skin. Now she was smelly and sodden, and Harry was even soggier.

'I guess it's just not my day,' she told the wide-eyed Maddy and the almost pop-eyed cattlemen. 'Some days you just shouldn't get out of bed in the morning, and this is one of them.'

'Bryony!'

Uh-oh...

Bryony turned cautiously to find her friend, Myrna McPherson, watching her from the pavilion door. Myrna had her six-week-old twins inside a pushchair; Peter, aged five, was clinging to one side of the babies and Fiona, aged six, was holding the other side of the pushchair handle. All of them were gazing at Bryony as if she'd taken leave of her senses.

'Hi...' Bryony faltered, and started to laugh again.

Myrna didn't laugh. She regarded her friend with resigned horror, as if Bryony had done something dreadful, but what did she expect? This was Bryony, after all.

'There are sheep loose all over the fairground,' Myrna said carefully, ignoring Bryony's laughter. 'Someone said a little grey dog was chasing them. Would that be Harry, then?'

'Hmm.' Bryony stopped chuckling and met her friend's look with a guilty smile. 'It might be.'

'I see.' Myrna rolled her eyes. 'You don't think you could have held on to him?'

'I got distracted.' Bryony didn't say with what, or with whom, and by the look in Myrna's eyes she didn't need to. Myrna was a very good friend.

Now she was focusing on something other than the disgusting Bryony and her even more disgusting dog. She'd spotted the child at Bryony's side and she smiled a welcome.

'Hi, Maddy.'

'H-hi.' Maddy's thumb came up and wedged into her mouth, and she backed imperceptibly behind Bryony.

Bryony could feel the fear. She frowned, feeling as protective as a mother hen. A sodden, smelly mother hen.

'Do you two know each other?' Bryony asked, looking from Maddy to Myrna.

'Maddy's in the same class as Fiona at school.' Myrna gave her small daughter a gentle push forward. 'Say hi to Maddy, Fiona.'

Maddy dived completely behind Bryony, and Myrna's eyes widened.

She looked at Bryony, her eyes asking a question, and Bryony gave her head an almost imperceptible shake. *Don't push it.*

Myrna was anything but stupid; she got the message loud and clear. She put a restraining hand on Fiona's shoulder, stopping her daughter from walking forward.

'On second thoughts, go no further, Fi,' she ordered. 'Bryony stinks.'

Bryony glared. 'Gee, thanks.'

'What are friends for if they can't give each other gentle hints about body odour? You weren't thinking of going home in my car, were you?' They'd come together, packed like sardines in Myrna's small Fiat—four children, two adults and one dog.

'Well, yes...'

'Well, no.' Myrna screwed up her nose in distaste. 'I'd

have to sell the car if I let you near it, or your stink would mingle with the petrol fumes and blow us all up. Heaven knows what that chemical combination is.'

'But...'

'We were squashed before,' Myrna said definitely. 'And now...Bryony, that dog is definitely not coming in my car—and neither are you!'

'Myrna...' Bryony stared helplessly at her friend. 'You have to.'

'No, I don't.' There was a twinkle behind Myrna's eyes that said she was enjoying herself. 'I'll send Ian back for you with the truck.'

Ian was Myrna's husband, and Bryony was torn between laughter and dismay.

'Myrna...Ian's busy. Don't you dare.'

'Ian's sowing barley this afternoon.' Myrna gave Bryony her sweetest best-friend smile. 'But he'll be finished about six and I'll send him to fetch you then. I don't see what else you can do. The local taxi sure won't take you.' She screwed up her nose some more and looked around to where the farmer with the hose was spraying dung from the concrete floor. 'At least you're among your own kind here among the cows. I'll tell Ian just to follow his nose when he comes to find you, shall I?'

'Myrna, you rat...' Bryony took a hasty, laughing step forward and discovered Maddy was clinging to her leggings, tightly, dung and all. Myrna's eyes widened still further, but she made no comment.

'Come on, children,' Myrna told her troop, grinning widely and turning her pushchair with the air of a woman with purpose. 'Let's get out of here. Aunty Bryony has finally gone too far—and I don't want to stick around to see the consequences. I can see from here that they'll be far from pretty.'

With a last, mischievous chuckle, Myrna swept from the pavilion, leaving Bryony with Harry—and Maddy—until six o'clock... Two more hours. Oh, great. Two hours of wandering round the fairground looking and smelling like a pile of dung.

'Won't she take you home?' Maddy was still tucked safely in behind her, and her hand still clung.

'No. She won't.' Bryony sank down on a hay bale with Harry in her arms, and Maddy sat sympathetically beside her. 'Do you know what a fair-weather friend is, Maddy?'

'No.'

'That.' Bryony gestured to the departing Myrna's back. 'She's a great example. I come halfway around the world to rescue her business and she doesn't let me in her car because I smell a little.'

'You smell a lot,' Maddy said truthfully.

'Gee, thanks.'

'Jack'll take you home.'

Now that was a thought. Why hadn't that occurred to her? Bryony cringed inwardly at the prospect.

'I'll just bet your D—I'll bet your Jack drives a lovely new car with cream leather seats.'

'Sometimes he does, but today he's driving a truck. A big one, with little houses built on the back for the dogs.'

'Well, that's a possibility. Maybe I could use a dog house.' Bryony grinned down at Maddy and, to her delight, the child smiled back.

'Silly. You could sit up front with us. I'll go ask.'

Before Bryony could stop her, the child had slipped away and was racing nimbly around assorted cows and out of the pavilion door. She disappeared. Oh, help... Bryony rose, with Harry. Now what should she do?

Myrna had said Bryony was among her own kind here, and she was, up to a point. The pavilion was full of magnificently groomed cows and bulls and calves, and everything had the faint odour of dung. Here, if Bryony sat quietly on her hay bale and waited for Myrna's husband, she'd attract not much more than the odd disgusted glance.

But...

But she'd promised Jack she'd deliver Maddy back to

the dog-trial ground. Maddy was now on her own, and the trial ground was on the other side of the fairground. So there was nothing for it but to tuck Harry more firmly under the arm of her disgusting sweater and take off after her.

'Maddy, wait for me. Maddy…'

Bryony's boots weren't meant for running and Harry, although small, weighed a ton. Maddy beat her by a country mile. By the time Bryony puffed her way into the trial ground, Jack Morgan was listening to his daughter's tale with an expression on his face that told Bryony he was trying to conceal anger that she was alone. Bryony could tell at a glance that he was furious.

'I don't understand,' he was saying. The trial ground was deserted and, as Bryony reached the stands, she could hear every word. Then Jack looked across and saw her.

'Oh,' he said. 'Nice of you to join Maddy.' It was sarcasm at its most pointed.

'She ran ahead.' Bryony tried to glare, but it was hard to puff and glare all at the same time. She stopped where she was—twenty feet away—and concentrated on her glare-puff technique. Then she checked out Jack's disdainful glance and figured she didn't have to be there at all. She'd seen Maddy back. Even if she had to puff a bit more to leave, it was worth it. This man thought she was a cross between a caterpillar and a maw-worm.

'I'll see you later, Maddy,' she called between puffs. 'Maybe at the next dog show. Thanks for helping me find Harry.'

'Don't you dare be at the next dog show,' Jack growled, and even Maddy looked dismayed. But she grabbed her father's arm and pulled.

'No!' Her voice was urgent. 'I told you. We have to take Bryony home because she smells.'

She did smell, too. Jack remembered. She smelled really good.

'Honey…'

'The bad dog got cow muck all over her and then a man

sprayed her with the hose and now she and Harry smell so bad that Fiona's mummy won't take her in the car. Bryony has to sit with the cows until someone comes with a truck, and that won't be for ages and we have a truck.'

Jack stared down at his little daughter. Then, slowly, his eyes moved again to Bryony, and he registered what Maddy had been trying to tell him.

Bryony's hair was sodden. Her white clothes were stained green and disgusting. The dog in her arms was even worse. If he'd tried for the rest of his life to think of a suitable punishment for this woman, he couldn't have come up with a better one than this. She was foul.

Or maybe…maybe not quite. Bryony was mired and wet and out of breath, but she stood, her chin tilting with defiance and her green eyes flashing—and Jack thought suddenly that he'd never seen anything more beautiful. Or more ridiculous.

'She says she can go in one of the dog houses on the back of the truck, but she can come in the front of the truck with us, can't she, Jack?'

Jack's shoulders shook.

'Don't you dare laugh,' Bryony said carefully.

'Why not?' Jack's eyes twinkled with pure Machiavellian enjoyment. 'You appear to have met your just deserts.'

'Thank you.' Bryony spun on her heel.

'Miss Lester.'

Bryony ignored him. She stalked away, boots squelching water, and three seconds later was stopped by a large hand on her shoulder. She wheeled around and discovered Jack's wicked laughter directed straight down at her.

'Whew,' he said. 'I can see Fiona's mother's point of view.'

'Thank you,' she said, with as much dignity as a lady with an armload of manured dog could muster. It didn't help that Harry was wriggling fiercely, trying to get down to greet Jessica.

'Will this help?'

Jack produced a collar and lead from his pocket—Harry's. When Harry had slipped his collar, Bryony had dropped it as she'd tried to grab him back.

'Someone found it in the grandstand and gave it to me.' Ignoring the smell, Jack reached out and fastened the collar around Harry's neck. Harry raised his eyebrows, wriggled his backside, and looked eagerly down at Jessica, still standing obediently at Jack's side.

'Your taste in women might be impeccable, but your choice of aftershave leaves something to be desired,' Jack told him as he lowered Harry onto the ground with a ruffle behind his disreputable ears. The two dogs greeted each other with joy. Harry's choice of aftershave obviously suited Jessica down to the ground. Jack wasn't looking. He was looking at Bryony.

'Can we drive Bryony home?' Maddy's voice was urgent and entreating.

Jack frowned.

'Why?'

Blunt and to the point. Bryony couldn't think of a single reason why he should.

'Because I like Bryony,' Maddy said stubbornly. 'And it's not her fault Harry's bad.'

'He's not trained.'

'You could help train him,' Maddy said eagerly, but even Bryony thought that was going a bit too far.

'Thanks, Maddy,' she told the child. 'But I'll just go back to my cows and wait for Ian.'

Jack hesitated. 'Ian who?'

'McPherson.'

Jack's face cleared. For some reason, the thought of Bryony meeting a man he knew as safely married eased a tension he'd hardly been aware was building.

'Ian McPherson's sowing crop this afternoon,' he told her. 'I passed him on the way here.'

'I know,' Bryony said politely. 'But when he finishes he'll come and get me.'

'He won't finish until dusk.'

'Then I'll wait until dusk.'

Jack sighed and ran a hand through his hair, barely lifting his hat as he did.

The knot of tension tightened again. There was something about Bryony Lester that told him he should pick up Maddy and Jessica and leave now, have nothing more to do with her.

But Maddy was tugging his hand with an urgency he'd never seen in the child before.

'I like Bryony,' she'd said.

Well, he didn't like Bryony. A more useless, ornamental, smelly... She had great eyes. He didn't like women's eyes. He liked Bryony's. She had great legs. Ditto. Her hair was fabulous! Oh, brother...

'Come on,' he growled. 'I'll take you home.'

Bryony bit her lip. As an invitation it lacked some polish. She should refuse.

But she was wet and she stank—maybe it hadn't been such a good idea to be hosed down. Despite her run, she was now feeling just a bit cold, and promising to get colder.

'The offer's good for two minutes,' Jack said, seeing her look of reluctance. 'We're going home now. Take it or leave it.'

She didn't want to stay here for two more hours. Even if Jack Morgan was an arrogant toad he was a really good-looking arrogant toad. With a great smile... When he could be bothered to produce it. And he loved Maddy; even a fool could see that. So he couldn't be all bad. She managed a smile herself.

'Thank you,' she said submissively. 'I'd like to go home. Harry and I will sit on the back so the wind takes our smell backward.'

'No. I want you to sit in the front with me,' Maddy said stubbornly. 'We don't mind the smell—do we, Jack?'

'We might.' Jack's tone was cautious. 'In fact…'

'When we found that sick lamb last week I nursed it all the way back to the house in the front of the truck and it smelled horrid,' Maddy said hastily. 'You put it in the stove and it smelled all the time until it was warm enough to go back to its mother. My lamb was nice—but Bryony's better.'

She had a point there. Jack looked hard at Bryony and gave himself a swift mental shake. Get a hold on yourself here, boy! Get this over with. Fast.

'My truck's behind the grandstand,' he said bluntly, then he called his dog, took Maddy by the hand and strode off towards it, as if he couldn't care less whether Bryony followed or not. Which was about as far from the truth as it was possible to get.

The ensuing drive was tense, to say the least. At Maddy's insistence, Bryony sat inside the cab, but she was acutely aware that she smelled, that she was soaking the upholstery and that Jack Morgan thought she was some sort of bad joke low life.

Which, all in all, managed to put a stop to Bryony's normally cheerful chat.

The two dogs stayed in their enclosures on the truck tray and, by the end of the ride, Bryony would almost have preferred to be back there with them.

She gave brief directions to her cottage on the outskirts of town, then huddled herself and her aroma in the corner and concentrated fiercely on not moving. Every time she did, a fresh wave of dung wafted over the cabin. Jack had both windows down as far as they'd go, but even Maddy was looking uncomfortable by the time they pulled up. Bryony was out of the cabin door practically before the truck had ceased moving.

'Thank you very much for the ride,' she told them, managing another smile. They seemed to be getting harder. 'I'll just get Harry off the back…'

And then she stopped. Jack had carefully placed Jessica in one enclosure and Harry in another. Now they were lying in the one enclosure, side by side, and the pong wafted out from both of them. Jack jumped down from the cabin to help release Harry—and when he saw the dogs his jaw dropped a foot.

'What...?' he said, and his tone was back to being dangerous. 'Who...?'

'It wasn't me!' Bryony's voice was practically a yelp. 'They were in separate enclosures when I saw them last, I swear.'

'It was me.'

Maddy had hardly talked all the way home, answering Bryony's questions in monosyllables. Now she climbed carefully down from the cabin. She addressed Jack in an 'I cut down the cherry tree so pack me off to the colonies on bread and water' tone that made Bryony cringe. 'I did it while that man came over to talk to you after you'd put the dogs up,' she continued. 'Bryony was looking at you and no one was looking at the dogs and Jessica looked lonely.'

Jack closed his eyes, defeated. He would have liked to yell at Bryony, but he had to admit this wasn't her fault and he couldn't yell at Maddy. He could still be annoyed.

'Well, that's the end of Jess sleeping on your bed tonight, young lady. She'll smell almost as bad as Harry. We'll bathe her in the morning.'

Maddy's face fell, and Bryony had the sudden feeling that, for Maddy, maybe the colonies on bread and water were preferable to a night in bed without a dog.

'Hey, you can bathe her tonight,' she volunteered.

'She takes hours to dry,' Jack snapped.

'So use a hairdryer.'

Maddy and Jack both stared at Bryony as if she were talking a foreign language.

'A hairdryer?' Bryony looked from one to the other and frowned. 'You know—a neat little electric gadget that blows hot air on wet heads?'

Maddy looked doubtfully up at Jack. 'I don't think we have one of those—do we?'

'We don't.'

Bryony sighed.

Escape wasn't easy.

'Well, I have two,' she confessed. 'You'd better come in and we'll bathe Jess here. But I get first go at the hot water.'

'Two…?'

'Two hairdryers.'

Jack stared. 'Why on earth do you have two hairdryers?'

'In case you haven't noticed, I have rather an oversupply of hair.' Bryony grinned. 'I hold the hairdryers one on each side of my ears and my hair flies straight up like something out of *Star Wars*. It's a great sensation, and a lot quicker than using one.'

Jack had a sudden mental image of Bryony—fresh out of the shower—naked and glowing, with a hairdryer in each hand, red hair flying upward. He felt dizzy.

'I don't know…' His voice came from a long way away.

'Oh, stop quibbling. My dog has made your dog smell, so I'll fix it.' Bryony leaped lightly up onto the truck tray, released the dogs from their cage, then jumped down again and grabbed Maddy by the hand.

'Come on in,' she said cordially. 'If you give me ten minutes while I wash myself, then I'll wash both dogs and send you home with a sweet-smelling Jess and a clear conscience. It's the least I can do—and I always do the least I can do.'

She and Maddy marched forth, dogs following adoringly behind, and this time it was Jack who was left to follow, whether he liked it or not.

Bryony left the dogs outside and Jack and Maddy in her sitting room while she showered. By the time she emerged, Jack was starting to wonder just what sort of madhouse he'd got himself into.

Bryony's cottage was like no other he'd ever seen. From

the outside it was ordinary enough, though the two vast ceramic elephant legs—one on either side of the entrance—were a fair indication of what was to come.

And inside...

This lady was a chronic collector, a magpie, and what she collected was extraordinary. There were furnishings here from all over the world.

The furniture itself was huge—way too big for such a tiny cottage. The lounge sofa and chairs didn't match. Each was vast and overstuffed and in a different colour of some sort of vivid silk. A riot of huge, squashy cushions tumbled over them and onto the floor. The floor itself had about ten rugs, layered one on top of the other. Each was in a different fabric or texture and the effect was one of some sort of crazy comfort cocoon.

And the paintings...

Weird, wonderful paintings—some of which were astounding, some just plain beautiful and a couple...well, if Jack had his choice he'd turn them to the wall while Maddy was in the room.

And there were things... Sculptures, some big, some small. An array of glasses on the sideboard, none of them matching but each one individual and wonderful. Small tables of exotic wood, with seashells and carvings and strange-looking seed pods...

Maddy wandered about the room, open-mouthed, and Jack sank into one of the vast chairs and just plain stared. This lady was a nut! A complete, utter nut! What sort of person put eight rugs on a floor hardly big enough to hold one?

They heard her in the shower next door, making enough noise to suggest there were a couple of whales in the bathroom. She dropped the soap and they heard her attempts to pick it up with astonishment. Maddy got the giggles.

'Close your ears, Maddy,' Jack growled. 'You're not to learn those words.'

'She doesn't think we can hear.'

'No.'

Maddy found this extremely satisfactory. She checked out each seat, chose the highest and clambered into it. Definitely into. You didn't *sit* on any of Bryony's furniture, you sank.

'This is the best room…' Maddy sighed. 'You know you said we could decorate my room? I'd like my room just like this.' She giggled. 'Jack, take your hat off. See that horn? I think it's a hatstand.' She clambered off her seat, lifted Jack's hat from his head and took it over to place it on what looked like some sort of bugle, stuck on a bamboo pole. Ridiculous!

But Maddy was grinning, and she'd removed Jack's hat. For a child who only went near Jack when she had to, it was a beginning. Then Bryony burst back into the room, clad in jeans and an oversized white T-shirt that said 'No Fear' in huge red letters. Her amazing hair was turbaned up on her head in a white fluffy towel. She looked fresh and scrubbed and bare-toed—and absolutely gorgeous.

Jack blinked.

'Your house is wonderful,' Maddy told her before Bryony could speak. 'Is the rest like this?'

'Well, the rest is a bit crowded.'

'You mean this isn't?' Jack stared around in incredulity and Bryony grinned.

'I collect things. I have visions of one day living in a big house and needing all this. When I moved from New York I tried to sell a bit but selling things is okay in principle. It's only when you pick up each thing and look at it and remember where you found it that it gets impossible. And storing… I know I should put some of these rugs into storage, but they're sort of fun like this.'

'You brought all this from America? It must have cost you a fortune.'

'Mmm. But I couldn't leave it behind.' She grinned down at Maddy. 'Could I, now? Want to see my bed?'

'Oh, yes…' Maddy bounced across the room and grabbed Bryony's hands. 'Please…'

Bryony grinned at Jack. 'You can see it, too, if you're interested,' she offered. 'Otherwise, go grab a beer from the kitchen straight down the hall. I should have offered you one before I showered. I'm sorry. All I could think of was getting rid of my smell.'

Jack forgave her. Just like that. He got up in a daze and found himself not getting a beer but standing by Bryony's bedroom door staring in amazement at the bed.

It was vast, king-sized or bigger, carved in some sort of deep red wood—mahogany or something similar—with huge posts at each corner and all hung with gold and purple drapes—like something out of a sultan's palace.

'It's ridiculous.' Bryony chuckled. 'I'll have to sell this. Roger says he won't sleep in it in a fit and it's hardly a guest bed.'

'Roger?' Jack was finding it hard to catch his breath.

'My fiancé.'

A fiancé. Yeah, right. Jack managed to catch his breath on that one. For some reason, it made things seem more in control.

'I'd like to sleep in it,' Maddy announced, unaware that a spiral had just stopped mid-spin for Jack. 'Very, very much.'

'Well, if Jack says you can, then maybe one night you can spend the night with me and Harry.'

'Harry sleeps here, too?'

'Actually,' Bryony admitted, 'Harry and I swim in this bed. I told him he should really have been a giant wolf-hound just to fill it up. We thought of letting out pillow space.' She ruffled the little girl's pigtails, and Maddy, who normally cringed when touched, wiggled her head as if she thoroughly enjoyed being ruffled. 'Okay, miss. Let's cope with these dogs. Harry first because he's the worst. And then your Jess.'

*   *   *

What followed was a very silly hour. If anyone had ever told Jack he'd enjoy himself so much washing and blow-drying a couple of smelly dogs he would have thought them ridiculous. But Bryony had them all in fits of laughter. They ended up—all of them—back in her crazy sitting room, knee deep in rugs with damp dogs and hot air going everywhere.

The dogs thought it was wonderful and so did Maddy. Jack was just plain hornswoggled. Who the hell was Roger? Finally he could bear it no longer.

'So tell me,' he said as the overfluffed and pristine dogs rolled on the rugs with Bryony and Maddy. 'What the hell are you doing here in Hamilton? Is Roger a local?'

Bryony's laughter died a little.

'Roger lives in Sydney.'

'But…you're marrying Roger.'

'Not until next year.'

'I see,' he lied. He didn't see at all. 'But…presumably you came from New York to marry Roger?'

'Well, sort of.' Bryony grabbed a passing dog and started brushing. She sighed. 'Roger and I have known each other for ever. He proposed years ago, but I hadn't seen the world yet so I took off to America. I'm an interior designer.' She grinned. 'If you hadn't guessed.'

Silence. Bryony cast a swift look at Jack. He was frowning, and for some reason Bryony found herself fighting for words.

'I built up an interior design agency in New York, but I missed Australia,' she continued, talking too fast now. 'And Roger kept visiting and giving me all the good reasons I should marry him. And then Myrna—I met Myrna at university and we started in business together way back in the Dark Ages—wrote that she was having twins and her interior design business here would have to close if she couldn't find anyone to look after it for a while. So I figured I'd come home in stages. Twelve months living here getting used to not being in New York—and then Sydney and marriage to Roger.'

'But…I thought you were American.' Maddy didn't like this turn of events. Bryony moving on…Bryony an Australian…

'I'm half American,' Bryony told her. 'My mom was American, but she married my dad a long, long time ago and he's an Australian.'

'Oh.' Maddy's face cleared. 'You're still like me, then.'

'Yep.'

'But…you're going to live in Sydney?' The disappointment in Maddy's voice was poignant and Bryony reached to give her a hug. Jack stared. Maddy… Hugs…

'I'm not going to Sydney for yonks.'

'What's yonks?' Maddy asked, bewildered.

'Yonks is so far ahead I refuse to think about it.'

'Don't you want to marry Roger?'

'Sure I want to marry Roger.' Bryony's voice was defensive. 'He's cute.'

'So's Harry,' Jack said dryly, and Bryony grinned.

'Yeah, well, Roger has certain advantages over Harry.'

'What?' Maddy demanded.

Bryony's green eyes twinkled. 'Well, for a start he's a rich lawyer. He can keep me in the manner to which I wish to become accustomed.'

'Jack's rich,' Maddy retorted. 'You could marry him.'

Yeah, right. All of a sudden, the silence was loaded. Bryony scrambled to her feet. 'Tea,' she said. 'I'm starving. Are you?'

'Yes.' Maddy was definite, but Jack rose too, and took her hand.

'We have to go, Maddy.'

'I'm not offering a seven-course meal here,' Bryony told him, and grinned. 'I can't. Cooking is not my forté. I'm offering toasted cheese sandwiches.'

Maddy's face set into obstinacy. 'Cheese sandwiches are my favourite.'

Jack looked down at his small daughter and sighed. He shouldn't be here. This woman was beautiful. This woman was intelligent and funny. This woman was eccentric. This woman was engaged to another man.

He should get the hell out of here—right now.

But Maddy had come alive. His daughter had been with him for three months now and she'd been flat and listless and uninterested the whole time.

Bryony had made her laugh. You could forgive a lot of a woman who made your daughter laugh.

Besides, there was a part of Jack that wanted to spend more time here, wanted to sit on the other side of the kitchen table and watch Bryony make toasted cheese sandwiches—watch Bryony do anything...

'If you have enough bread and cheese,' Jack found himself saying weakly.

'I have enough to burn,' Bryony said cheerfully. 'And I hope that's not prophetic.'

CHAPTER THREE

So DID he stay for long?'

Monday morning. Time for Myrna and Bryony to get together and discuss Hamilton's interior decorating needs for the week. Myrna and Harry were on the couch; Bryony was disappearing under cushions on the floor. Interior decorating was taking a back seat.

'About four hours.'

Myrna shoved Harry's rump sideways—Harry went for warmth, and rump against thigh was his favourite feel—and regarded her friend with awe. 'Did you feed him?'

'Yep.'

'*What* did you feed him?' Myrna asked doubtfully. She knew Bryony's cooking.

'Toasted cheese sandwiches. I burned the first two lots. We fed them to the dogs and then Jack took over.'

Myrna stared.

'I don't believe it.'

'Don't believe I burned the sandwiches?'

'Well, of course I believe that. It's a wonder you haven't burned the whole house down by now. Your ability to not concentrate on your cooking is legendary. It's just... Bryony, *Jack Morgan*...'

'Why is it so amazing that Jack Morgan brought me home and visited my house and ate my cheese sandwiches?'

'Because he doesn't visit.'

'Doesn't visit who?'

'Doesn't visit anyone. The man's practically a recluse.' Myrna grinned. 'Well, with women, anyway. He has a *past*.'

'Don't we all?'

'Speak for yourself.' Myrna hugged her knees and looked around the room with affection. 'This place is great—and not a nappy in sight. I think I'll move in.'

'Uh-uh.' Bryony's curls shook. 'I'm off house-mates until next year. Harry's my chaperon. I'm practising being an engaged lady.'

'I imagine it must be a strange feeling, being engaged.' Myrna sighed. 'I wouldn't know. I was single and then— wham!—I was married. I can't remember anything about being engaged, except maybe the one morning Ian let me out of bed long enough to buy a wedding dress.'

'Yeah, well, that's why you have four kids and I have none. No self-control.'

'Not when Ian's in sight.' Myrna sighed again, happily, and hugged her knees tighter.

'You want a bucket of cold water dumped over you? Hey, Myrna?'

Myrna gave herself a shake, lost her cat-got-the-cream look, and mock-glared at Bryony. 'You don't feel this way about Roger? Like you only have to look at him and your knees turn to jelly?'

Bryony thought. 'I guess. I mean, I suppose I do. Roger looks great in his Italian suits. Smooth.'

'But does he look great *not* in his Italian suits?' Myrna grinned. 'The first time I saw Ian I had him undressed in my head in two minutes flat. Or less...' And then she fixed Bryony with a look. 'You always fall for suits. I don't understand it.'

'I love good-quality suits.'

'So do a deal with Armani, buy yourself a suit and hang it in your wardrobe. And then get on with the important things in life. Like finding a *man*! Heck, Bryony, you had Jack Morgan in your house last night. How can *that* compare to a suit? Bryony, Jack Morgan is seriously sexy.'

'He is, isn't he?' Bryony fiddled with her coffee mug,

and blushed. Myrna looked at her sideways—looked
again—and decided to ignore the blush. For now.

Myrna, comfortably plump and pretty, and gloriously
happy with her Ian, wasn't all that impressed with Bryony's
Roger. This had definite promise, but she knew better than
to push.

'So what gives with Maddy?' she asked, carefully changing the subject.

'Now there's something I don't understand. Maddy. Tell
me about her,' Bryony demanded. 'That little girl has seen
trouble.'

'Well, you're right there. She's disturbed enough.'

'So tell me why.'

'I'm not sure.' Myrna sighed. 'Well, maybe I do know
a bit. Maddy was born here.'

'What—in Australia? I thought she was American.'

'Her mother was from the States. Or maybe...more cos-
mopolitan, if you like. Georgia always made out she had
contacts everywhere. Jack met her overseas when he was
quite young, married her in the States and brought her here.
Only she hated the farm, hated Australia. In the end she
hated Jack. She whinged until we were all sick to death of
her. She had Maddy and then, when the baby was about
three months old, she skipped the country, taking Maddy
with her.'

Bryony frowned. 'Jack didn't want his daughter?'

'Jack wasn't given the choice. He went away for a weekend to some important farming conference and when he got
back they'd gone. He went to the States looking for them
and there was talk he was trying to get custody, but he
didn't succeed.'

'But he found her?'

'I don't know. All I know is that he came back here and
buried himself in his work. Absolutely. The loss devastated
him and he compensated by making money. Jack has one
of the most profitable sheep studs in the country, and for a
sideline he breeds and trains sheepdogs. His dogs are leg-

endary. Jack Morgan is seriously rich, but he doesn't enjoy a cent of it. Bitter, that's what Jack is, isolated by choice. Then three months ago Maddy arrived.'

'To stay?'

'As far as we know. Jack's not talking. And Maddy... Well, she won't talk to anyone or go near anyone if she can help it. She goes to school, but she keeps to herself. Her teachers are at their wits' end because she won't communicate. I was stunned she was touching you yesterday.'

'Mmm.'

Bryony thought back to the last time she'd seen the little girl, at ten o'clock last night. They'd played Scrabble on the rugs. Bryony had lost against the combined team of Jack and Maddy—for heaven's sake, what sort of man knew a *xyster* was an instrument for scraping bones?—and then Bryony had walked out to the truck with them to say goodbye. Maddy had placed her arms round Bryony's neck and clung. She was a little girl in need.

'Will you see her again?' Myrna asked carefully. She knew better than to ask whether Bryony was seeing Jack again. After all, despite Myrna's disapproval, Bryony Lester was an engaged lady.

'Yes.'

'Yes, when?'

'This afternoon,' Bryony told her, and blushed all over. She glared up at Myrna. 'And it's not what you're thinking, it's work.'

'Don't tell me you talked Jack Morgan into redecorating?' Myrna looked hopeful. 'Jack's place is vast. We get a job like that and we can retire. Set up in the Bahamas.'

'With or without your twins?' Bryony shook her head. 'No. Luckily for the twins and your Ian, it's only Maddy's bedroom. It seems it's sparse and Jack's trying to get her interested in re-doing it. Only she isn't. Then last night she said she wanted a bedroom just like mine.'

'Like yours?' Myrna's face went blank. 'You mean...she saw your bedroom?'

'Yes.'

'Did Jack see your bedroom?'

'Yes.'

'You did tell him you were engaged?' Myrna demanded, suddenly anxious, and Bryony laughed.

'Yes again, goose.'

'If he's seen that bedroom, he has the wrong idea about you,' Myrna said gloomily, and Bryony thought about it.

'No. Every girl should have a bed like mine.'

'If every girl had a bed like yours, the production of this country would hit zero, except for kids. Bryony, you must be nuts. He'll think you're sex-starved...'

'Why, for heaven's sake?'

'Bryony, you have black satin sheets! I have never known anyone with black satin sheets, except someone with a red light on their front door. It's a good thing Maddy was there, otherwise you deserved to be ravished on the spot.'

'I wouldn't mind!' For the life of her, Bryony couldn't keep the wistful note out of her voice. 'The odd spot of ravish by Jack Morgan might be rather fun.'

'Bryony!'

'Okay, okay.' Bryony held up her hands, laughing. 'I know. I'm engaged to Roger. But I haven't seen Roger for a month, and being engaged doesn't stop me looking.'

'Wanting?'

Bryony appeared to consider. 'Well, if he is seriously rich...'

Myrna threw a cushion at her. 'Bryony Lester, I know what you sold your agency for in New York. If you want the Bahamas, there's nothing stopping you. And Roger's not exactly poor...'

'There's nothing to stop a girl wanting more.'

'So join the spider-widow club. Marry serially and poison them off as you go, starting with Roger and working through every eligible bachelor in the country.' She grinned and threw another cushion. 'Bryony, get these indecent thoughts right out of your head and let's get to work.'

*   *   *

Which was all very well, but the indecent thoughts just wouldn't go. Bryony gave herself severe lectures all day, but all they did was give her more excuses to think of Jack.

Jack's smile.

Jack's body.

Jack's hands...

She was having hot flushes on hot flushes and she was engaged to Roger.

'So get out there, plan Maddy's bedroom and get the heck out of their lives,' she told herself severely.

Jack's home was a rambling homestead, huge and solid, with verandahs running right round and a fragrant, over-grown garden teeming with birdlife, poppies and roses. Spreading English oaks grew on the boundaries of the home garden. Set amidst wide paddocks dotted with river gums and grazing sheep, and with the river running on its northern boundary, the whole place looked like paradise.

Bryony was met by Maddy, who'd clearly been waiting for her. The child led her through the house to the kitchen, and by the time they reached it Bryony's nose had told her that paradise was just where she was.

'Jack's made gem scones,' Maddy said anxiously. 'Do you like them?'

'Do I like them?' Bryony shook her head. 'Gem scones! I haven't eaten them since my grandma made them when I was a little girl. No, Maddy. I don't like them. I *love* them. And they love me.' Then she frowned. 'Did you say Jack made them?'

'He did.' Maddy appeared desperately anxious to impress. 'And he made the jam, too. Strawberry. There's bought stuff if you want, like my grandma used to buy.' She gave Bryony a look of entreaty. 'But Jack gets a bit funny if you eat bought stuff instead of his.'

'I don't blame him.' Bryony laughed.

Maddy swung open the kitchen door and the first sight of Bryony that Jack had was of her laughing, which was just how he remembered her. He'd been taking the gem scones out of the oven. Now he straightened, turned to put the griddle down on the sink and tried to smile. It didn't quite come off.

She took his breath away. Literally. Today Bryony was wearing a soft blue skirt that almost reached her ankles and a tiny white knit top, high-necked but with no sleeves. Her fiery curls tumbled down to her shoulders, her arms were slim and lovely, her face was creased into laughter and her green eyes twinkled. All in all, it was as much as Jack could do not to drop the griddle on his boots.

'Hi.'

'Hi.'

For two mature people it was a pretty limited conversation. Jack tried again. 'Did you have trouble finding the place?'

'No. But I thought...' Bryony was stammering. 'I thought... Myrna said you bred sheepdogs. There's only Jess...'

This was an improvement. He could think of something to say on this one.

'Were you expecting rows of battery dogs?' Jack's mouth curved into a smile. 'No. I employ a few men on the place and each of my men looks after a dog or two. That way they all have individual attention. I have a breeding programme, but in every other respect they're my men's dogs. But Jess is mine.'

'Oh. I—I see.' Bryony stared down at the gem scones Jack was now flipping out of the griddle and wrapping in a cloth. Her eyes widened. 'Did you say...did Maddy say you made these?'

'Mmm.' Morgan, there *has* to be a better conversation starter than this! He was tongue-tied again.

'And the jam?'

'That's right.' Not much better.

'Do you want to plan my bedroom and then eat scones, or will you eat the gem scones first?' Maddy asked anxiously, and Bryony sat down at the kitchen table and reached for a plate.

'Both,' she said promptly, and relaxed. She looked up at Jack and gave him her very widest smile. 'A man who can cook! I'd like to know where you were when I was accepting marriage proposals,' she told him. 'Roger's starting to look distinctly second-rate.'

The only problem was—it was true. Bryony had said it as a joke, but as Jack walked by her side up the stairs to Maddy's room she was so aware of him that she felt the need for Myrna's bucket of cold water.

He was so big. So...so masculine. Roger smelled of expensive aftershave. Jack smelled...well, Jack smelled of Jack. Roger always looked immaculately groomed. Jack's shirt had a rip in the sleeve above where he'd rolled the sleeves up, and his jeans were old and stained.

Bryony was starting to be breathless, and it had nothing to do with the stairs. Concentrate on work, she told herself fiercely. Desperately. Then leave. Fast. But she was needed here, for Maddy's room was indeed sparse. Bleak would be a better word for it. Bryony stopped at the doorway and stared in dismay.

For a little girl's room, it was pathetic. Oh, it was a nice enough room. Beige walls. Brown carpet. Beige bedspread. One window facing north with a great view over the sheep paddocks to the river beyond. That was its one redeeming feature. But there was not a toy in sight. Not a stuffed animal. Nothing to suggest this was a child's room.

On the chair was one small battered suitcase. Full to bursting. On impulse Bryony walked over and pulled open the bureau drawer. Empty. The child had her suitcase packed, ready to go.

'Diana suggested we paint the room pink and buy Maddy some new clothes,' Jack said, and Bryony heard the desperation in his voice. 'But Maddy won't have a bar of it.'

'Diana?'

'My next-door neighbour.'

'I don't like pink,' Maddy said stubbornly. 'And I don't like Diana.'

Fair enough.

'I've never been a pink person myself.' Bryony considered. She walked over to the bed, sat and bounced.

'Okay, we have a start here,' she said. 'This bed is squashy. Squashy is good.'

'It's bad for backs.' Jack braced his shoulders. 'Diana said we should replace it.'

'Squishy's great.' Bryony fixed Jack with a look of defiance, bounced again, and her blue skirt flounced with her. 'Squishy's cuddly, especially if you're lonely. And squashy bounces.' Once again she bounced. Maddy couldn't resist. She walked over and sat beside Bryony—and gave a small bounce herself.

'I like squashy too,' she announced in a small voice that echoed Bryony's defiance.

'My bed's squishy,' Bryony stated, as if that clinched things. The two of them were a united, bouncing front, and Jack retired from the lists, defeated.

'Squashy can stay.'

Yes!

'Your bed's wonderful,' Maddy told Bryony wistfully, and Bryony looked around her, deep in thought.

'You know, if Jack built up the posts at each end of the bed, we could make your bed like mine. Smaller, of course—but pretty much a miniature copy.'

'You're kidding,' Jack said faintly.

'No, honest.' Bryony gave another bounce. 'We could order purple silk shantung—' then she took pity on him '—or satin if we're talking limited budget—and build a canopy. We could get a softer mauve lace and hang it over the sides, and have huge purple bows holding the satin back. Then you'd be sleeping at night in a wonderful purple tent.'

'Wow,' said Maddy.

'And you need a gold quilt,' Bryony continued. 'I know where we can get one that would look great. It has blue stars on a gold background. And we could paint the walls a softer gold and have a tiny purple and blue frieze running all around.'

'What…?' Jack was flabbergasted.

But Bryony wasn't to be stopped.

'This carpet has to go,' she ordered, looking with distaste at the murky brown. 'I'm sorry, but ugh.'

'Diana chose that carpet. It's very practical.'

'I'm sure it is, but bedrooms aren't meant to be practical. If Diana likes it, then give it to Diana. We need a really rich cream with gold fleck. And thick. We're talking shag-pile here, something you can dig your toes into and get a grip. And we need some pictures. That's harder. You'll have to help me choose, Maddy. Tell me what you like. What about a chandelier?'

'What's a chandelier?' Maddy demanded, riveted.

'Lights with diamonds,' Bryony told her. 'Hundreds of diamonds. And pale blue and cream curtains with gold sashes. Then we'll get those stick-on fluorescent stars to put on the ceiling so when you lie in bed at night you've got something to look at. What do you think?'

There was no need for Maddy to tell either Jack or Bryony what she thought. Her eyes were like saucers. What next? Bryony looked at the suitcase sitting forlornly on the chair. Hmm.

'I don't want to unpack,' Maddy said, seeing where she was looking.

'No. I understand that.' Bryony frowned. 'But brown doesn't go with purple. Hey, I think I know the answer. Have you ever seen ships' trunks?'

'Ships…'

'They're like a giant suitcase, only when you stand them on their side they turn into a chest with lots of drawers. You're packed all the time, even when you're opening and shutting drawers. We could get one made with lovely soft leather and have your name embossed on the side in big gold letters: *'Maddy Morgan'*. So when you go home to visit your mom you don't have to pack. You can just pick it up and take it with you.'

'I...I...' Maddy was speechless. So was Jack. He was staring at Bryony as if he couldn't believe his eyes.

'Am I talking too much money here?' Bryony asked, suddenly anxious. Myrna had said he was rich—and if ever money needed to be spent this was the time. 'I can get some of this stuff at fairly basic cost and we can find a second-hand ship's trunk. I'll do you a costing and you can work out what you want to do from there.'

'What do you want to do, Maddy?' Jack asked faintly. 'You didn't even want to paint your bedroom pink. Do you like Bryony's ideas for your bedroom?'

'A furry floor?' Maddy asked slowly.

'Shagpile carpet,' Bryony said positively. 'Apart from layers of rugs, it's the only way to fly.'

'And...diamonds in my light?'

'A chandelier.' Bryony took pity on Jack. 'You get them made in glass,' she said kindly. 'It won't cost you as much as you think.'

'Do you think Jessica would still like to sleep in here if we change it?' Maddy asked anxiously, and Jack's lips twitched.

'I can't see why not.' He looked around for his dog. 'By the way—where is Jess?'

'Harry came with me.' Bryony gave him an apologetic smile. 'They're in the garden together. I made sure all the gates were shut so they can't get out.'

'You brought...'

'Harry loves Jessica,' Bryony said defensively. 'And he hasn't got any other dog friends.'

'I wonder why not?'

'There's no need to be rude about my dog.' She hauled a tape measure out of her pocket. 'Now, if you like

Maddy's and my plans, Mr Morgan, be so good as to hold the end of my tape while I get down some vital statistics.'

'We're not ordering yet,' Jack told her, still rattled.

'I understand that.' Bryony gave him her sweetest, most professional smile. 'I'll take my list away and do a complete costing for you. Then it's up to you to order or not.'

'But we pay for your advice anyway?'

'No.' It was her turn to snap. 'Maddy's my friend so I give advice free. You can take my ideas and do it yourselves. I'll even help paint if you want me to. If you order what you need through us, there's a ten per cent cost, but you can say goodbye to me now and it won't cost you a cent.'

He could.

Both Maddy and Bryony were looking at him. There was anxiety in Maddy's eyes—and he thought he could detect just a trace of it in Bryony's.

'I'll tell you what,' he said nobly. 'Let's get this measuring done and discuss it over the leftover gem scones.'

Bryony's heart-warming smile flashed out and she gave a triumphant bounce on the squashy bed.

'Sounds good to me!'

Somehow the gem scones didn't last long enough for all the discussion they had to do. Bryony rose to go and Jack found himself trying to think of a reason why she should stay, and Maddy gave him one.

'Let's show Bryony the farm,' she said urgently. 'We could take the horses out. Bryony, can you ride?'

'I can ride...' But then Bryony paused, mid-sentence. Jack was staring at his daughter in amazement.

'But you don't like the horses, Maddy.'

'I don't like the pony Diana told me I had to ride,' Maddy retorted. 'She's fat and she doesn't want to go and when you try to pat her she bites.'

'Diana brought her over so you could learn to ride.'

'I don't like her.' It wasn't clear whether Maddy was

talking about Diana or the pony. 'I already know how to ride. I like that nice little grey mare you call Jezebel.'

'Jezebel...?' Jack shook his head, thoroughly confused. 'Maddy, Jezebel's spirited and fast and—'

'I know. She's really pretty and she likes me.'

'But... Have you ever ridden a horse like Jezebel?'

He knew nothing about his daughter, Bryony realised with a shock. Nothing.

'Grandma gave me a horse like Jezebel when I was four. Her name was Fleece and she was lovely.' Maddy's voice went blank. 'I rode her and rode her, but when Grandma died my mom said Fleece had to be sold.'

Jack frowned. 'Were you and your mom living with your grandma when she died?'

You could have heard a pin drop. Bryony was aware that she hadn't breathed for the last minute, and she still didn't want to. Was this the first time Jack was finding out *any-thing* about his small daughter?

'No.' Maddy shook her head. 'Grandma and me lived by ourselves on Grandma's farm for as long as I can remember. Mom used to visit us sometimes, but Grandma said it was just when she wanted money. Then Grandma died and Mom said I had to live with you now, because she wasn't going to be saddled with a b—'

'Maddy!' That was Bryony. She couldn't bear Maddy to go on, but Maddy did.

'Mom said she'd won anyway—she'd taken me away from you and proved a point, and it would serve you right to be landed with me now when you didn't want me any more. She said she hoped I gave you hell.'

'Your mom said I didn't want you?' Jack's voice was raw and jagged.

'Yes.' Defiance. Maddy put her hands behind her back and faced him, chin tilted, as though expecting to be struck, and Jack could bear it no longer. He hauled the child up into his arms, held her stiff little body close, and buried his face in her hair.

'Maddy, when you were born I was the proudest man in the country,' he told her, his voice muffled. 'And when your mom took you to America I nearly went crazy. I spent years looking for you, but your mom never let me near.'

Maddy's body was still stiff. Jack sighed and put her down on a chair beside Bryony.

'Maddy, your mom was a dancer,' he told her. 'A beautiful ballet dancer. The best. Only then she damaged her leg and she couldn't dance any more, so she decided if she couldn't dance then she might as well get married—and that was a bad reason for getting married. She was angry that she couldn't dance and she was angry at everyone because of it. She even started to be angry at me, so she took you away. But Maddy, that *didn't* mean I didn't want you. I've told you over and over, and I'm telling you now. There wasn't a morning I didn't wake up and wonder where my little girl was. And the day your mom rang up and said you were on the plane coming here was the best day of my life.'

Jack took her small hands in his and looked straight into her fearful eyes.

'That's the truth, Maddy,' he told her gently. 'You're my little girl and you always will be.'

Maddy stared and stared at him and her eyes were almost drowning in his. There was still doubt. She was still fearful to believe. She turned to Bryony, her eyes pleading. Tell me what to do, her eyes demanded. Oh, help, Bryony thought desperately. What do I say to this?

But desperation bred inspiration. There were two dogs' noses pressed against the screen door. Jessica and Harry were avidly interested in the proceedings, and all of a sudden Bryony knew just what she had to say.

'You know, Maddy, Jessica loves your daddy very much.' Bryony managed a smile at the confused little girl. 'And I've always believed that dogs know best. Jessica thinks your daddy is the best thing on two legs, and I'm sure Jessica would tell you he'd never lie to you.'

Bryony's smile grew.

'And, Maddy, I think if Jessica could speak she'd tell you that you have a daddy who loves you. Absolutely. For ever.'

Maddy's eyes widened. She looked from Bryony to Jessica, and then she turned back to Jack. She considered, and she came to a decision. Slowly she reached forward and touched his cheek. That was all. But it was enough. Jack gathered her close. And Bryony burst into tears.

After that, they found a couple of large handkerchiefs to mop up Bryony, then ate the rest of the gem scones and went for a ride. Bryony wouldn't be left behind for quids. Her skirt was totally unsuitable for riding, so she simply ruched it up in her knickers and rode with loops of blue fabric hanging down. Luckily the horse Jack found for her was quiet.

Maddy's wasn't.

The mare she'd asked to ride was frisky and out for fun, but Jack had enough sense to let her try. Maddy swung herself onto the mare's back with the ease of a practised horsewoman, gave a whoop of sheer joy and took off down the paddocks to the river. Jack and Bryony were left sitting astride their horses, together, staring after the child in delight.

They could have taken off after Maddy, but both adults sensed Maddy's need for space. There was only so much emotion a child could take at a time. So they trotted easily in her direction. The sun was warm on Bryony's face, she was acutely aware of the man by her side and she'd never felt so happy or alive in all her life.

It was because of Maddy, she told herself, but she knew that wasn't all of it. It was because Jack was beside her, looking at her as if she'd personally produced miracles. All very satisfactory. Well, it would have been satisfactory if there hadn't been the small niggle of conscience that was screaming 'Roger'!

Oh, dear...

She urged her horse to a canter and off she flew, and Jack was behind her. She put her head into the wind—it was *so* good being on a horse again after all those years in New York—and all she could hear was the pounding of hooves underneath and behind her, and all she could feel was the warmth of the horse between her thighs with the feel of the wind in her hair.

Jack cantered on behind her, and the expression on his face was one of a man who didn't know what the hell he was seeing.

Maddy beat them to the river bank by a mile. By the time they got there, she was sitting on a fallen log, mid-stream, gazing longingly at the water.

'We should have brought our swimming things.'

Bryony dismounted and walked down to the sandy shore. She kicked off her sandals and walked in up to her knees. Her skirt was still ruched up around her, like medieval pantaloons.

'Ouch!' She winced and hopped on one foot. 'It's cold.'

'I don't mind cold,' Maddy said wistfully. 'It looks lovely.'

'Is it safe?'

Jack was still on horseback. He looked down from the back of his wonderful black stallion and smiled benignly.

'Safer than a beach. Come back and swim some day.'

'It'd be nice now,' Maddy said.

So it would. Cold but nice.

'Come on in, then,' Bryony called—and dived neatly under. It was indeed cold! She broke the surface to find man and child looking at her as if she'd taken leave of her senses.

'You're all dressed.' Maddy was pop-eyed.

'Yep.' Bryony rolled over onto her back and kicked her toes, sending up a spray of water.

'Your skirt...'

'Is too heavy,' Bryony had to agree. She fiddled under the surface, managed to undo the buttons and slipped right out of it. 'Lucky my knickers are respectable. They're more respectable than my bikini.' She held up her skirt for some-one to take. For Jack to take.

'I can imagine,' Jack said dryly, trying to suppress a grin. He dismounted, tethered the horses together and then came onto Maddy's log, lifting Bryony's skirt from her grasp. 'Shall I take care of it for you?'

'If you would.' Bryony smiled up at him—blushed—and then dived under the surface again. After the initial chill, the water was gorgeous.

'I want to go in too.' Maddy was practically hopping up and down on her log with excitement.

'It's cold in there,' Jack warned her.

'Bryony will take care of me.'

Jack stared down at his daughter and his face twisted into an unreadable expression. Then he came to a decision.

He hauled off his shirt and then helped Maddy off with her dungarees.

'Come on, then, Maddy,' he told his daughter, his voice firm. 'We'll both take care of you.'

CHAPTER FOUR

THEY rode back to the house at dusk, tired, wet and muddy but thoroughly content. Bryony couldn't remember when she'd enjoyed herself more as she led Maddy's little mare. Jack had his daughter up before him on his stallion. Maddy's small frame was nestled against his chest and the expression on Jack's face was one of peace. She'd achieved something here, Bryony thought. Something wonderful.

There was a Range Rover parked next to Bryony's car and a woman coming down the verandah steps to meet them. The woman was around thirty years old, slim, and was wearing cream linen trousers and blouse, with pearls. She had beautifully bobbed hair with sunglasses perched on top, even though the glare from the sun had long since faded.

'Jack...'

Then she saw Bryony and stopped.

This wasn't the way she would want people to meet her, Bryony thought ruefully. She'd put her skirt back on—sort of. It hung limply round her knees. Her hair hung in sodden, curling strands down her back and she was aware there was river reed mixed up in there somewhere. And there was mud on her face...

'Hi, Diana.' Jack swung himself down from his horse and lifted his daughter down after him. He held her in his arms, cradling her as if she were an infant, and Maddy was too tired to object. Or maybe she didn't want to. It was as if she'd been fighting her need for caring for months—years—and had now given in to it.

'I wondered where you were.' Diana appeared not to notice the child.

'We've been at the river.' Jack motioned to Bryony. 'Diana, this is Bryony Lester, Hamilton's newest interior designer. Bryony, my neighbour, Diana Collins.'

Bryony tried a muddy smile. 'Hello.'

There was no answering hello from Diana. She was staring at Bryony in stunned amazement.

'I read about you... In *New Interiors*. I was going to ask you to see my place...'

Was... Past tense. Whoops, thought Bryony. Myrna would *not* be pleased. She really had to do something about her image.

'I heard Maddy wasn't at school today.' Diana turned back to Jack, excluding Bryony nicely. 'I came over to see if anything was wrong.'

'Nothing's wrong.' Jack smiled down into his daughter's sleepy face. 'Maddy's been designing her bedroom with Bryony. A purple and gold bedroom...'

Diana frowned. 'I thought we'd agreed we'd paint it pink.'

We. There was some sort of proprietorship here.

'Bryony has other ideas.'

She certainly did. Bryony was staring in consternation at the pedestrian gate into the garden.

'Jack, the gate's open.' Bryony swung down from her horse, tethered it to the fence and walked fast through into the garden. 'Harry... Harry...'

'If you mean a fat little grey mutt, he streaked out with Jessica just as soon as I opened the gate,' Diana told them.

Oh, no...

'He is not fat,' Bryony said automatically, but her mind wasn't on diets.

'There's no problem, is there?' Diana was saccharine-sweet. 'I mean...Jack's dogs don't chase sheep.'

Harry might. In fact, going on past record, if Harry saw a sheep he probably would. With a sigh, Bryony went back to her horse.

'I'll have to go find him,' she told Jack. 'I'll be back as soon as I can.'

'Let me come with you.' It was Maddy. She stirred in Jack's arms and struggled to get down. Jack set her on her feet.

'You need a bath,' Diana told her, distaste in her voice. 'Jack and I will give you one while—'

'I'm going with Bryony.' Sleep was forgotten. Maddy was definite.

Jack sighed and smiled and swung himself back on his horse, then held out his arms so Maddy could come up before him again.

'Sorry, Diana. Seems we're off on a dog chase.' His smile died. 'If he's chasing sheep...'

Bryony cringed. She'd spent time on a sheep farm as a child. She knew what dogs among the sheep could mean.

'I can't stay,' Diana warned.

'That's a shame,' Jack said. Bryony didn't think it was a shame at all, but Jack obviously thought so. 'I'll ring you later.'

Diana was left staring after them.

Harry was indeed chasing sheep. They saw the sheep first—a vast mob drifting around the far paddock in a panicking mass. Bryony had seen this before. Once, when she'd been small and visiting relations on a farm, her uncle had taken the gun out when the home dogs had started barking. Bryony had followed at a distance. She'd seen the sheep panicking like this. And then she'd seen a pack of three strange dogs—and a dozen dead and maimed sheep. Her uncle had shot the dogs.

'Please...please...'

A small dog could do as much damage as a big dog. If Harry was killing, then Jack could demand he be put down. And if Jessica was with him...

'Call Jessica,' Bryony said urgently, but Jack shook his head.

'I want to see what she's doing.'

If she was killing, then he wanted to know. He urged his horse on and Bryony was left behind. The light was fading fast. She reached the top of the hill and strained to see... And stared. There was no sheep-killing here.

Instead, there was one tiny mob of sheep in the middle of the paddock and the bigger mob was milling around the boundaries. Jess was guarding the smaller mob. She lay crouched—almost flat—eyeing each sheep within her cluster.

But, out of the corner of her eye, Jessica watched Harry. Harry was moving into the main mob, cutting out individual sheep and driving them into Jessie's smaller cluster. For heaven's sake... It looked as if Jessica was teaching Harry to round up the sheep—and they were having a ball.

Bryony's mouth fell open. She dared a glance at Jack, expecting anger, but all she saw was astonishment.

'Well, I'll be damned.' Jack ran his hand through his river-damp curls. 'I've never seen anything like this in my life before. She's got more than a dozen sheep now. Look, he's bringing in another one.'

And Harry nudged and worried the heels of his next victim, driving the ewe into Jessie's mob. Then he looked at Jess, as if for approval—and raced back to fetch another one.

For a sheepdog, he looked ridiculous. Maybe he was fat, Bryony conceded. But he could move...

Jack was laughing, hugging Maddy tight as the little girl laughed with him, and watching every move the dog made.

'You know, I could make a sheepdog out of Harry.' Jack grinned. 'No sweat.'

Maddy straightened in her father's arms. 'You mean...train him...?'

'Well...'

'You could, couldn't you?' Maddy insisted. 'You could help Bryony and she could come here all the time...'

'Hey, whoa...'

This needed some thinking about. Jack gave a piercing whistle, Jess looked up and saw her master—and abandoned her game in an instant. The collie streaked up the hill to Jack, and, with a last reluctant look at the sheep, Harry followed.

Both dogs greeted their owners with joy. Jess stayed by Jack's horse, but Bryony was taking no chances with Harry. She swung out of her saddle, gathered her dog to her and hopped back up again.

'You can stay out of trouble up here.'

Harry looked adoringly up at her and wriggled all over, shivering with excitement. For a city dog he was having the time of his life.

'How long have you had him?' Jack asked, watching as the schnauzer settled himself into Bryony's arms.

'Two months.'

'Two months.' Jack frowned. 'He's not a young dog.'

'I saw him in a pet shop window.' Bryony stroked her mischief-prone dog with love. 'He has a pedigree a mile long, but his past owners said he was too much trouble.' She frowned. 'I think they hit him. For the first couple of weeks after I got him, every time I raised my voice or took a fast step toward him he went and hid under the bed. He sat in the pet shop for a month before anyone would buy him.'

'And then along came you...'

'I couldn't leave him there,' Bryony said defiantly. 'Besides, he was reduced.'

'I'll bet. Reduced in price, but not in waistline.'

'There's no need to be rude about my dog.' She wheeled her horse. 'I'm going home.'

'Would you like me to make you some dinner first?'

Afterwards Jack could never figure out why he'd said it. He hadn't meant to. It just sort of slipped out all by itself.

Bryony considered. Myrna would find out, she thought. Myrna had been expecting Bryony back by five. Myrna would be climbing walls by now, but not with worry. Roger had said he'd ring at seven...

'I'd love dinner,' Bryony said, and she heard the defiance in her voice with a sense of guilt.

Oh, dear... What was she getting into now?

There was chicken pie for dinner, courtesy of Jack.

'I do a huge cook every Sunday,' Jack explained, seeing Bryony's look of absolute astonishment when he hauled the pie out of the refrigerator.

'You mean...you made this?'

'I made it.'

'Marry me,' Bryony said—so promptly that Jack laughed.

'I imagine your Roger might have something to say about that.'

'Yeah, well, he'd better learn to cook. This is serious.' Bryony promptly forgot Roger and considered her bare toes. 'But before I eat...I don't suppose... Can I borrow a shirt and jeans?'

'You'll swim in my clothes.'

'I'm still swimming in these,' she confessed. Her skirt was damp and distinctly unpleasant around her legs 'I'm sure there are porrywiggles down my back.' She peered down at Maddy. 'And I'll bet Maddy has porrywiggles, too. Can we have a shower to get rid of all the little wriggly things, please, sir, while you go about your domestic chores?'

'You're serious about the jeans and shirt?'

'Do you have a waist-length piece of baling twine to hold everything up?'

'That can be arranged.'

'You're a man in a million, Jack Morgan,' Bryony said devoutly. 'Maddy Morgan, you hold onto your Daddy because he's worth a mint!'

* * *

Jack put his pie in the oven, had a fast shower himself, then started a salad, listening all the time to the noises in the girls' bathroom.

Maddy was in the bath and Bryony was through the partition in the guest shower and they sounded as if they were having a ball. Jack had to give himself a sharp inward kick. Surely he wasn't jealous! He couldn't resist. Abandoning his salad, he strode along the corridor to listen.

'They took a lofty whaling ship
To Greenland's icy shore...'

Bryony was singing at the top of her lungs. She had a lovely rich contralto voice, helped along by steam.

She paused. 'Come on, Maddy,' she ordered. 'It's a great song, but it needs volume. I've told you the words. I'll splash cold water over you if you don't. So sing!'

Jack held his breath. And Maddy sang.

'We thought we'd take a school of whales...
While we were outward bound, brave boys...'

The volume hit maximum and Jack retired to the kitchen, stunned. Bryony was like a bomb blast, he thought. A bomb blast erupting in his life with fragments of order going everywhere.

She was a beautiful bomb blast. A bomb blast who was engaged to another man. Just as well. He did not—*did not*—want a woman in his life, ever again.

Maddy needed a mother.

Well, maybe she did, but if he had to remarry he'd marry with his head this time. Someone sensible. Someone like Diana. You knew where you were with Diana; she had the same values, the same sensible purpose. A working partner.

Would Diana sing whaling songs in the bath?

Fat chance.

Jack tossed his salad and grinned and found himself singing along. His deep baritone sounded down the corridor and, in their respective bath and shower, the girls heard and chuckled in delight.

'No more, no more Greenland for you, brave boys.
No more, no more Greenland for you.'

Bryony looked even more wonderful in Jack's jeans and shirt than she did in her own clothes, if that was possible. They hung on her like rags but the twine held everything in at the waist, the shirt billowed to her thighs and her curls looked fantastic when they were wet.

It was as much as Jack could do to keep his eyes off her all through dinner. It was lucky dinner didn't last long. Maddy was almost asleep in her pie.

'Come on, chicken,' Jack said as she finally drank the last of her milk. 'Bed.'

'I don't want to go to bed.'

Every night the same story. Every night there was a tantrum. It was as if the night was frightening.

I'll just bet it is, Bryony thought. How would she have felt to be packed off halfway round the world when she was six to a father she'd never known except as an ogre?

'How about if I tell you a story?' Bryony rose and held out her hand. 'I know a great story. I read it to Harry every night. I don't have the book here—tomorrow you can come and borrow it and see the pictures—but I know it off by heart.'

'You read a book to Harry?'

'How's he ever going to learn to read if I don't?'

Maddy's terror receded. She giggled.

'You're silly.'

'So everyone tells me. Can I tell you my story?'

'Will Harry listen?'

'Harry, and Jessica too.' They were outside with a marrow bone apiece. Bryony crossed to the back door and called them in.

'And me?' Jack's voice was almost anxious.

She didn't know about that. Bryony looked at Jack with an expression that was suddenly doubtful, but Maddy nodded.

'All of us. In my bedroom that's going to be purple.'

There was no arguing with that. So three minutes later Maddy was between sheets, a dog under each arm and two grown-ups at her bedside, while Bryony told the story of *Harry the Dirty Dog*.

It was a children's classic by Gene Zion. Bryony had fallen for it in a big way the first time she'd read it, and Maddy loved it. Or she loved half of it.

The exertions of the day had taken their toll on the child—and on the dogs, too. By the time *Harry the Dirty Dog* was uncovered from his mud and reunited with his family in his happy ending, Maddy, Jessica and Harry were all fast asleep. Bryony's voice faded to a close.

She stood—and found Jack standing, too, only inches away, and he was smiling at her with an expression in his eyes that did strange things to her insides.

'Thank you, Bryony,' he said softly. 'You've performed miracles.'

'Wait till you see the bill for the purple bedroom.'

She smiled. Keep it light... She looked down at Harry, curled up beside Jessica on the coverlet. One of Maddy's hands was on each dog.

'It seems a shame to move him.'

'Leave him. I'll bring him to your cottage tomorrow after I take Maddy to school.'

There it was, he thought, stunned at his own brilliance. A wonderful excuse to call. Cut it out, Jack!

'I... Thank you...'

Bryony took a step towards the door. A step closer to Jack. And looked up at him. They'd turned the main light off, and there was only the sliver of light from the child's bedlamp casting a soft glow over the room.

Jack's face was all shadow—and all wonder. Bryony looked up in mute query. It was too much. Too much for any man. Against his better judgement—against anything he'd ever told himself these last six years—Jack Morgan moved as if in a trance and took Bryony Lester in his arms.

Bryony froze. Just for a moment. Just for that split second before his hands came around her and hauled her against him and the warmth flooded through her body as if she were suffering internal combustion.

His mouth came down on hers.

She made a sound like a whimper and a plea—and then something happened in her brain to stop everything but the sensation of this man holding her. He was so big. So powerful... His shirt was rough against her hands and the hairs of his arms caressed hers. His mouth was wide, mobile and demanding—wanting her—tasting her—possessing—and suddenly all Bryony wanted to do was be possessed.

He was so... He was so Jack!

He was all around her. She was cradled against him, her breasts crushed against his chest and his feet against her bare toes. Then his tongue was sliding into her mouth and she forgot her feet, forgot her breasts, forgot everything except the fire inside that was growing by the second.

Dear God, she wanted this man. This man was like no other. Her hands clutched at the back of his shirt, wanting him closer. Her mouth parted so he could taste all of her and she could taste him. Jack...

'Woof!'

For the first time in his life, Harry decided to try out as guard dog. Or just try out as one jealous male protecting his territory. He stood on Maddy's coverlet and gave a hesitant woof—apologetic but firm.

Excuse me, this is inappropriate behaviour and you're interrupting something very important—like my sleep!

And Bryony burst out laughing within the confines of Jack's arms.

'You dopey dog.' Then, as Harry lowered his haunches into attack position, she leaned hastily forward. 'No! You'll wake Maddy.'

Jack laughed and shook his head, still holding her tight against him. 'I wouldn't worry. Nothing short of an earthquake will wake Maddy.'

Then he looked reluctantly down at her—and he let her go.

'Harry's right, though.' His voice was slurred with desire, but common sense was breaking through. 'This is crazy. You're engaged.'

So she was. Why hadn't she thought of that?

'I...'

'And I don't want any involvement here. It's stupid.' He took a step back.

'Funny. I thought you wanted it very much.'

'I don't make love to women.'

Bryony frowned, trying to fight internal fires, trying not to reach out and touch him again. 'And that makes me...?'

'No.' He took another step back. It was as if he was scared of how she was making him react. 'No.'

'Okay, then.'

Bryony shook her head, trying to clear the fog. 'Okay. Harry says we're stupid, so we're stupid. I guess this is where I butt out.' She looked down at Jack's clothes she was wearing. 'I'll collect my wet clothes and go. You still want to keep my dog overnight?' Duty done, Harry had slumped back down on the bed, fast asleep in seconds.

'Yeah. If Maddy wakes...'

Sense aside, he still wanted to see this woman in the morning.

'Fine. You can collect your clothes then.'

He'd never wash them again.

Bryony looked uncertainly up at him—and then stood on

tiptoes and gave him a light kiss on the lips. A kiss of farewell.

'Don't take this hard, Jack Morgan,' she said firmly, in a way she was far from feeling. 'Hey, it was only a kiss.'

But both of them knew that it wasn't.

'You're engaged to Roger and you kissed Jack Morgan. Bryony Lester, are you out of your mind?' Myrna's voice down the phone was a squeak of stupefaction.

'Yeah, well…'

'Was it good? Does he kiss as well as I think he'd kiss?'

'Better.'

Bryony's reply was instantaneous. She was curled up on her couch. It was ten at night and she'd only just got home, but Myrna had been calling every ten minutes since six.

'I don't believe this. He took you horse-riding and gave you dinner and kissed you.'

'Yep.'

'And you kissed him back?' It was a squeak again.

Bryony considered.

'Yep.'

'Are you out of your tiny, flea-brained mind? How on earth are you going to marry Roger now?'

'It didn't mean anything.' Bryony wriggled uncomfortably. 'I mean…it was only a kiss.'

'Bryony…'

'Look, he kissed me. It's hardly the end of the world.'

Myrna sighed as if she was stupid.

'Bryony. Sweetheart. I'm not accusing you of unfaithfulness here. I'm not about to ring Roger and tell all. What I'm saying is…how can you kiss Jack Morgan—and marry *Roger*?' And Myrna's voice was so full of loathing as she said Roger's name that Bryony burst out laughing.

'Oh, for heaven's sake… Myrna, Roger's sweet.'

'So's that horrid fruit you buy in the tropics—durian— once you get past the smell. So they tell me. Personally, I don't want to ever get near enough to try.'

'Myrna, Roger's been faithful for years…'

'Yes, and that's something else that worries me.' Myrna was away in full flight now and there was no stopping her. 'You haven't been faithful to Roger for years, right?'

'I've only been engaged for two months.'

'So… For years you've been happily sowing wild oats all over New York…all over the world…and faithful old Roger sits at home bleating that you're the only one. Bryony, either the man is seriously stupid or he's a liar. Either way, I don't like it.'

'Has it ever occurred to you that he might love me?'

'Since you were kids in school together? When you were in New York for years and he wasn't? And how often did he call? About once a month—when he suddenly remembered he was madly, truly, passionately in love and needed to propose again. The truth is, Bryony, you're the first wife he thought of and our Roger is seriously lacking in the imagination department.'

'Myrna, this is none of your business.'

'No. It's not. But if you're wandering round the country letting men like Jack Morgan kiss you…' She sighed. 'Bryony, wake up. Get a life. And move in on Jack Morgan like there's no tomorrow.'

Bryony let that run round her head for a minute. She wriggled her toes on the floor, instinctively looking for Harry as toe-warmer—and then remembered where he was. And that Jack was bringing him home in the morning.

'Myrna, even if I was interested, there's a lady called Diana…'

'Diana Collins?'

'That's the one.'

'Hmm.' Myrna was silent for a minute. 'I'd heard that Diana was interested—but until now Jack's never reciprocated.'

'She's definitely proprietorial. And also superior.'

'She's good at superior.' Myrna sighed. 'I always meet Diana down the street when my eyeliner's smudged or one of the twins has sicked milk on my shoulder. She looks at me like I'm something to be pitied. Every time I meet her I have to race home and have Ian hug me and tell me I'm beautiful. You want to compete with Diana, then you'll have to do something about your magnetic attraction to cow dung.'

'Yeah, well, I don't know whether I do want to compete with Diana.' Bryony hitched her feet under her again and chewed her lip. 'Myrna, let me think about this one for a while, will you? Give me some space.'

'You've got space.' Bryony could hear Myrna's smile down the phone. 'The twins need a feed so for now you've got space. But don't think I'm giving up on this one, Bryony Lester, you have me seriously interested. You and Jack Morgan… Well, well, well!'

CHAPTER FIVE

MYRNA might be seriously interested—but was Bryony?

It was a long time before Bryony got to sleep that night. She lay in her vast, canopied bed and, for the first time since she'd bought it, the bed felt lonely.

It was because Harry wasn't there, she told herself, but she knew it wasn't that. She'd had this bed in New York, where she hadn't had a dog. And lonely wasn't on her agenda. It never had been, she thought. Bryony had been an independent child, raised by parents who loved her but encouraged her to spread her wings early.

She'd met Roger at her first school dance. Roger had danced with the ten-year-old Bryony twice and announced she was the girl he'd marry.

He could well be right. Roger Harper was intelligent, considerate and good-looking, and Bryony never felt a need to argue with him. There was nothing to argue over. She'd dated other men, but Roger hadn't minded. He'd stayed solid and dependably in the background while he built his career as a corporate lawyer, and she'd returned to him when no one else more interesting was offering.

Marriage to Roger had finally achieved a feeling of inevitability. She'd refused to be engaged when she left for New York, rightly figuring she'd have more fun if she wasn't sporting a diamond. Roger hadn't objected even then, but he'd contacted her regularly through the years and reaffirmed his undying love.

For which she was grateful. She'd taken chances she might not have otherwise—spread her wings further—because she'd always had a safety net underneath her.

Roger.

Roger had given her years of absentee faithfulness. Then Myrna's letter had arrived, announcing she was having twins and her decorating business would crumble without someone to care for it. New York was winter-cold and the agency wasn't providing new challenges. Everyone wanted black, white and chrome—a look Bryony hated.

Two days after Myrna's letter had arrived—a day filled with sleet and traffic fumes and dreadful clients—Roger had arrived in person. He'd been faithful for years and it was time they were properly engaged, he'd told her. For once, Roger had put the pressure on, and it had seemed only fair to say yes.

Roger...

Bryony tried to conjure up his image, but all she could see was the Italian suits he was so darned proud of. So was she. She did like his suits. 'Buy yourself a suit and hang it in your wardrobe,' Myrna had said, and Bryony grinned ruefully into the darkness. Maybe Myrna had a point.

But the thought wasn't fair. She couldn't dump a perfectly good fiancé—a perfectly good future—just because one man had kissed her. One man... Jack Morgan. Drat him.

With decision, Bryony snapped on her bedlight, crossed to the bureau and fetched her one and only pair of flannel pyjamas. A couple of mothballs fell out of their folds as she lifted them from the drawer.

She'd been sleeping naked on her satin sheets—a sensation she just loved—but she couldn't sleep like that and think of Jack Morgan at the same time. She'd go stark staring crazy!

She'd bought the pyjamas when she'd visited friends in Alaska two years ago. The pink flannel made her feel about as sexy as a lukewarm hot-water bottle. Which was how she had to make herself feel now.

Right, Bryony!

She looked at the photograph on the top of her bureau and Roger smirked back at her from his silver frame. As if he were smirking at her flannels. Would Roger wear Italian-made flannel pyjamas? Maybe he would.

What about Jack?

She would be willing to bet a mint on Jack Morgan wearing no pyjamas at all. Good grief! She hauled on her pyjamas and did the buttons up to the neck.

Roger was still smirking. Funny how Bryony hadn't seen that in his smile until now. Like... 'You're wearing those flannel pyjamas just for me...'

Bryony stuck out her tongue at her beloved and turned his picture to the wall.

'And you can stay there until I've sorted me out,' she told him defiantly. 'I think I'm in serious trouble here.'

Four miles away, Jack Morgan was having the same sort of trouble. Sleep wouldn't come. Finally he threw back the bedcovers, put on a pair of jeans—Bryony had been right in her guess about pyjamas—and took himself outside. As he opened the screen door, two shadowy figures launched themselves out of the darkness and joined him.

Harry and Jessica.

'Okay, guys. I wanted to be alone, but if you promise not to talk too much...'

They promised. The grass was wet underfoot. Jack was barefoot and bare-chested and the night was cool, but he welcomed the chill. The dogs fell in beside him, one on each side, and Jessica looked up at him in concern.

'Okay, I'm hot, all right?' Jack told her.

The concern in her big brown eyes didn't fade and Jack fondled her under her ears. Harry moved around and gave Jess a lick on the nose, sharing her worry.

Jess reciprocated by licking Harry—and then licking Jack. The dogs were becoming inseparable, which was ridiculous.

'This is one unsuitable male for you, Jess, girl,' Jack told her severely.

Jess licked Harry again.

'Yeah, well...' Jack kicked a tuft of grass and his toe hurt. He welcomed the twinge of pain. He welcomed anything that took his mind off the heat in his body. How the hell to get his mind off one fire-headed girl...?

He sat down on the wet grass—then lay down on his back. The dew was cold on his naked skin, but he welcomed it. Both dogs looked at him as if he was crazy.

'That's what she'd do,' Jack explained. 'You have a problem? Then fix it and ask questions later. I'm hot, so I'll lie in the wet grass. Bryony would. How many women do you know, if they got cow dung on their clothes, would ask someone to hose them down? In public?'

Nobody answered.

'Hell!'

Jack dug himself deeper into the wet grass. The dogs flopped down beside him. They couldn't understand, but they could sympathise.

'I've been here before.' Jack groaned. 'In lust. That's what this is. She's just the most gorgeous thing...'

But he'd thought that about Georgia. His ex-wife.

Jack forced his thoughts back to the night he'd seen his wife for the first time. He'd been staying in the States with friends, and they'd announced they were going to the ballet. And Jack, who'd never been to the ballet in his life, had gone with them and seen Georgia. One of the party had known her, seen Jack's look of stunned admiration and introduced them after the show.

Georgia was simply the most exquisite creature Jack had ever met. Laughing and full of fun and nervous energy... And tiny. Not like Bryony. Bryony must be five-eight, five-nine...

'They're the same, though,' Jack said out loud.

Jack had been twenty-five when he'd met Georgia and he'd asked her to marry him on the second meeting. She'd refused because of her career, and he'd come back to Australia, disconsolate. Then, twelve months later, she'd contacted him. She'd hurt her leg. Her dancing career was over and if he still wanted to marry her...

Of course he had.

But he was crazy to have done such a thing. Georgia hadn't belonged here. She'd been like an exotic fish out of her tropical waters. She'd grieved for her dancing career and the limelight and adulation she'd enjoyed for so long, and Jack had become the focus of her grief. The cause...

Then she'd become pregnant and she'd hated the baby even more. By the time she'd left, there had been no love left between Georgia and Jack, only an overwhelming bitterness on her part, and sadness on his.

She'd been so twisted in grief for her lost life that she'd been past thinking logically. She'd known she could hurt Jack more if she took Maddy with her.

Six dreadful years...

'So I'm not about to start thinking of another exotic woman,' Jack told himself savagely now. 'Georgia was happy and bubbly and I thought she was gorgeous when we first met.

'She wasn't like Bryony.'

As he said Bryony's name out loud, an image of her rose before him. Bryony coated in manure and sodden and laughing—Bryony diving fully clothed into the river— Bryony on a horse, her hair flying free.

Bryony sitting by Maddy's bedside telling his daughter the story of *Harry the Dirty Dog*, her voice gentle and her eyes loving. Bryony's lips on his...

'A cold shower...'

Jack stood up, shaking the two dogs into wakefulness. 'Sorry, guys, I need a cold shower. I need ice—like, a glacier of ice—but a cold shower will have to do.'

He strode to the door and looked back. The two dogs had their heads to one side, ears pricked, puzzled.

'If there's ever going to be another woman around here, it'll be someone sane and sensible and accustomed to a place like this,' he told them firmly. 'Someone like Diana.

She's lived next door all her life. She's never going to
decide to go back to New York or turn into someone I don't
know.'

Diana...

Bryony!

Go take a cold shower!

Next morning Jack knocked on Bryony's front door with
his expression businesslike and efficient. He was here to
hand back Harry, place an order for Maddy's bedroom and
get out of here fast. His resolution lasted a whole two seconds.

Bryony opened the door like a miniature whirlwind and
all Jack could think of was fire.

She was scarlet. Scarlet and hot pink. Someone somewhere had surely said red and pink didn't go together.
Whoever said that hadn't met Bryony.

She was wearing some sort of amazing culottes—sheer
silky trousers that bagged out and came in to hang in vast
folds around her ankles. They were transparent, pink and
red like a sunset, and were lined with a deeper crimson that
shone through the transparent outer material as an inner
flame.

She was also wearing a tiny, pink, gold-buttoned blouse
that came not quite to her waist. There were a good two
inches of bare skin under her breasts and a gold chain belt
hung almost to the floor. Her blazing hair was hanging free;
she wore about five gold bangles on each arm and her toenails were purple.

Jack blinked.

Before he could take a breath—and he sure needed to
breathe—Bryony had grabbed him and was hauling him
towards the kitchen. She had an armload of excited schnauzer—Harry hadn't hesitated in his greeting—but one hand
was extended from under her dog to tow him inside.

'You're just in time. Myrna and I have made the *best*
pancakes...'

'*You've* made…?'

Bryony heard the misgivings in his tone and grinned.

'Well, Myrna made them. I supervised.' She hauled him on down the passage, laughing. 'Do you like my pants? I feel like something out of an Arabian bottle. For some reason I woke feeling lousy this morning—maybe it was missing Harry—so I dressed bright. Myrna came over and she says clothes don't help—only food—so we thought we'd try both. But she's made enough pancakes to feed an army and the twins, of course, aren't eating solids yet.'

She pushed him into the kitchen and Jack stopped short at the door, suddenly embarrassed. He didn't socialise. He hadn't socialised for six years. To sit and eat breakfast with two women, a pram full of twins and a schnauzer…

'Do you know Myrna? Great. Where's Jessica?' Bryony wasn't giving him time for second thoughts. 'In the truck? Oh, Jack… Myrna, give the man some pancakes while I bring in his dog. Jess deserves a pancake, too.'

She was gone—a ball of fire flaming her way out of the door.

Jack was left with Myrna. They eyed each other with extreme caution. Myrna was the first to smile.

'You know, you'll have to eat a pancake,' she said cautiously. 'It's often quicker with Bryony just to give in and do what she wants and then get on with your life afterwards.'

'She's a domineering…'

'Oh, no.' Jack had said the words almost under his breath but Myrna had heard the criticism and jumped straight to her friend's defence. She gave Jack another shy smile. 'She seems… Sometimes she seems a bit over the top, but that's usually when she's nervous.'

'She's nervous now?'

Myrna met his look. And held it.

'Yes.'

Silence for a whole five seconds. Myrna checked him out from the toes up. She'd seen this man from a distance.

He'd always seemed cold and aloof, but Ian said he was a
great mate, and those words were the best accolade Ian
could give a man. He said Jack's wife had been... Well,
Myrna couldn't repeat things like that even in her head. So
Myrna could forgive the *aloof*.

And he was wearing faded jeans and a shirt without
sleeves. Boy, did he have great arms! Not a suit in sight.
Her smile suddenly grew as bright as Bryony's.

'Have a pancake,' she said warmly, and parked a plate
in front of him.

Jack's eyes widened. Come into the parlour, said the spi-
der... Myrna saw the thought and laughed.

'Hey, we won't eat you,' she chuckled. Then, as Bryony
walked back through the door with both Harry and Jess
adoringly at her heels, she looked up at Bryony and
grinned.

'Go and cover your toenails,' she ordered. 'You're scaring Mr Morgan to death and I gather he's a client. I'm your
boss. Go put a twin set on.'

'A twin set?'

'Or a jacket. Something businesslike.'

'Are you here on business?' Bryony ignored the order
and sat down at the table, reaching for her half-eaten stack.
She was continuing right where she'd left off.

Jack took a hold on himself. His reaction to this woman
was crazy. She might have the power to take his breath
away—but Bryony just kept concentrating on her pancakes.
Myrna had said she was nervous. Ha! There was only one
person in this room who was nervous.

'Maddy and I talked about her room on the way to school
this morning,' he told her.

'Mmm?' He was lucky to get that from Bryony. It was
hard for her to say anything at all when her mouth was full
of maple syrup and pancake.

'We'd like you to go ahead.'

Bryony nodded and finished another mouthful. 'That's

great, but hang on. We haven't given you the costing yet. Myrna and I were just figuring it out when you arrived.'

'Have you finished it now?'

Bryony hauled the pad and pen from in front of Myrna. 'Yep. Ballpark figure...'

She told him a sum that made him blink.

'That's if we do everything using professionals and make the hangings with silk shantung,' she told him. And then she smiled, taking pity on the man. He had the look of a man who could use a little pity. 'We always give the bad news first. That's the most expensive materials and having everything—painting and sewing—done by outsiders. If you paint yourself...if we use satin instead of silk...and if I do the sewing...'

'You?'

'Yep. Sure. I can sew.' Bryony smiled at his look of disbelief. 'If you'll let me, I'd like to do it. It can be a welcome-to-Australia gift to Maddy, from me.'

Jack continued to look stunned and Myrna slipped another couple of pancakes onto his plate, then placed two on the floor—one apiece to the dogs.

'Bryony *can* sew, you know,' Myrna said kindly. She was starting to feel quite motherly towards this man. 'She's not completely useless. She may not be able to cook...'

'I can cook!'

'Oh, yeah?' Myrna fixed Bryony with a look. 'What can you cook?'

Bryony thought fast. 'Toast?'

'Only if I fix the setting on the toaster for you.' Myrna gave her friend a sardonic grin and turned back to Jack. 'Anyway, the figure's much more reasonable if you do the painting and Bryony sews and we use satin,' she told him. And she named a figure that was half the first.

Jack ate half a pancake while he thought. He was stunned almost to silence—but not by the costs they were throwing at him. These two women... He'd never known anything like this. They were warm and funny and friendly and their friendship radiated outwards like a warm glow. He hadn't known women could be like this. Maybe he didn't really know women.

All of a sudden he had a vision of his own kitchen back at the farm...his kitchen as it could be...filled with women and babies and dogs... Holy heck... He ate another pancake while Bryony made a fuss of the dogs and fed them more pancakes.

Harry's sides almost visibly swelled.

'Jessica doesn't eat anything unless I feed it to her,' Jack said suddenly—sharply—as if he'd just remembered, and Jess looked up reproachfully and returned her attention to her pancake.

One of the twins woke and squawked. Myrna lifted the baby from the pram, opened her blouse and let the baby have what he wanted. If things got much more domestic, Jack would drown. He rose from his chair so fast he knocked it over, and both women looked up at him in surprise.

'Does this bother you?' Myrna asked, motioning down to the feeding baby.

'No. Of course not...'

'It shouldn't.' Bryony was on the defensive fast. Myrna was always welcome to feed her babies in Bryony's kitchen, and if Jack didn't like it he could lump it!

'I'm sorry... I should have asked...' Myrna turned slightly away from him, embarrassed. 'I assumed you'd have grown accustomed when your wife fed Maddy...'

Georgia had never fed Maddy, Jack thought bitterly. Not in a pink fit! To breast-feed babies might damage her figure. And she didn't like babies, anyway. It was Jack who'd coped with bottles and formula and two a.m. feeds. But that didn't mean the sight of breast-feeding bothered him.

Or maybe it did. It made him hungry. Hungry with a desire that he'd never known he had. For a woman... For this. For peace and friendship and laughter, and a kitchen that was all a home... So marry Diana! Marry someone sensible.

'Look, it really doesn't bother me—but I do have to go,' he said, and his voice was strained. 'We'd like you to go ahead with the bedroom, though.'

'Which option?' Bryony asked, watching him with eyes that were puzzled. 'Do you want to paint the room yourself? Do you trust me to sew?'

'I'll paint.' He managed a smile. 'And I'd appreciate it very much if you sewed. Maddy... Well, it would seem more special to Maddy if you helped. But...'

'But?'

'But I'd like you to order the silk shantung,' he said definitely. 'Maddy wants a bedroom like yours and I don't think the satin would be as good.'

'I don't think so either,' Bryony said warmly. 'But the shantung costs a bomb.'

'It'll be a cheap bomb if it makes her happy.'

Bryony smiled, instantly warming to the concern behind his words. Because of it, she forgave him for embarrassing Myrna. Her brilliant smile reached out and caressed him—and tugged him into a thrall so deep that he felt the need for a cold shower all over again. How many cold showers could one man have in a day?

'How about the pictures and ship's chest?' Bryony asked. Myrna had subsided into gently rocking her son as she nursed, and was content to watch rather than join in the talk. Bryony hesitated. 'You know, it would be ideal if Maddy could come to Melbourne and choose them herself.' Her smile became a bit unsure. 'If you'd let me, I'd love to take her.'

Jack knew that Maddy would love to go, and if anyone could make his small daughter smile this woman could. But it was Jack's turn to hesitate.

It was a wonderful, generous offer for Bryony to take Maddy to Melbourne, but all of a sudden he couldn't bear it. Maddy and Bryony... Maddy and Bryony—and not him.

'Only if I come too,' he growled, and then he blinked.

Good grief! What on earth had he just said? He sounded like a kid missing out on a treat. And he hated the city!

'You want us all to go to Melbourne?' Bryony's smile faded. 'But... It's an overnight trip.'

'I know that. We can stay at the Windsor. I'll pay for us all.'

Myrna's head shot up from her baby and she stared. The Windsor... Whew...

'When do you want to go?' Myrna asked cautiously. Bryony was looking too dumbfounded to speak.

'Whenever Bryony can.' Jack turned to Bryony. 'Bryony?'

'Bryony?' Myrna repeated. Nothing was getting through. No answer at all. Myrna gave her friend a swift kick under the table. 'Bryony, the man's asking you a question.'

Bryony gulped. Was this a good idea? Bryony wasn't the least bit sure, but...but it didn't seem there was a choice here. She'd made the offer to take Maddy to Melbourne. She could hardly tell Jack he wasn't welcome to join them. Especially if he put her up at the Windsor.

She fought for professionalism and grabbed her appointment book.

When...?

'Next...next Monday and Tuesday?' She looked at Myrna. 'Are those two days okay with you? Can you man the phone and put appointments off till I get back?'

'It's fine by me,' Myrna said. She was staring from Jack to Bryony with absolute bemusement. 'Don't mind me at all. I'll fit in.'

She was babbling.

'Okay, let's do it!' Bryony grabbed a pen and wrote it in big black letters before anyone could change their mind.

'Jack and Maddy. Melbourne.'

Then she frowned. 'Is it okay if Maddy misses school again? She missed yesterday.'

'Well, I guess if she misses three days of first grade she

may not make the college of her choice,' Jack said gravely.
'But what the heck? Let's live dangerously.'

What the heck, indeed. Let's live dangerously?

'I must be out of my tiny mind!'

As the door closed behind Jack and Jessica, Bryony put
her face on the table and head-banged.

'You'll get maple syrup in your hair.'

'Well, I've got batter for a brain, so it'll match. Oh,
Myrna, what on earth have I done?'

'You've accepted a date to go to Melbourne with Jack
Morgan; that's what you've done.' Myrna placed her sleeping son back in the pram and started clearing plates. 'I
thought it was a bit unwise myself...'

'"It's fine by me..."' Bryony parroted her friend perfectly. 'If you thought it was unwise, why didn't you tell
me I couldn't go? That you couldn't look after the phone?'

'I can.'

'You could have lied!'

'You're a big girl now. You can protect yourself—and
besides, you want to go.'

'I don't.'

'Codswallop.' Myrna shoved the dishes in the sink and
turned back to her friend. 'There. I've made you pancakes
but the washing-up's yours.' She sighed and her voice gen-
tled. 'Bryony, why have you shown the man your bed,
kissed him and dressed like you've escaped from someone's harem if you're not interested in him? Tell me that!'

'I'm not interested in Jack Morgan!'

'Bryony...'

'I'm not.'

Myrna fixed her with a look.

'Bryony, are you sure? Did you paint your toenails purple just for me, now? Or did you do it for him?'

'I don't know,' Bryony wailed. She caught Harry round
his ample midriff, hoisted him up onto her lap, and hugged.
'Harry, I just don't know...'

'You do know. He's a lovely man.'

'He's a chauvinist.' Bryony forced away the vision of Jack as a lovely man and concentrated on imperfection. 'He didn't like you breast-feeding Luke.'

'He did.' Myrna smiled—a placid, maternal, Mona Lisa smile. 'It was a shock, that's all. I guess his wife didn't feed Maddy and he hadn't seen it before, but he was pretty much taken with the idea.'

'Pervert...'

'No.' Myrna shook her head positively. 'Despite what the prudes tell us, most men don't see breast-feeding like that. They like it, but it makes them feel protective and paternal themselves, and that's what Jack was starting to feel. Like he wanted someone of his own doing just that—feeding his baby.'

'How on earth do you know?'

'Women's intuition,' Myrna said infuriatingly, and Bryony grimaced.

'Yeah, right...'

'Seriously, Bryony, the man's getting that nesting feel. I can sense it a mile off.'

'Just lucky he has Diana, then.'

'He kissed *you*. He's going to Melbourne with *you*.'

'I'm engaged to Roger.'

'Well, you know, if I were you, I'd do something about that,' Myrna said helpfully. 'Soon. Being engaged to Roger might get in the way of all sorts of things.'

'Myrna...'

'Just a suggestion.' Myrna arched her eyebrows at her friend as she hauled the pushchair into the doorway, ready to leave. 'Because deep down I love you and I want what's best for you. You're my very favourite friend. I'm off now. It'll give you time to think. But you and Harry have a good old discussion while I'm gone.'

Bryony glared. 'About what?'

'About whether you want to spend the rest of your life married to a good-looking suit with the personality of a flatfish—or whether you want to take a chance on Jack Morgan.'

CHAPTER SIX

MONDAY came way too fast and Bryony wasn't ready.

She was still engaged to Roger. He'd phoned on Sunday afternoon and afterwards she couldn't even remember what they'd talked about.

Something about Roger's mother buying them china for a wedding present, she thought—oh, and Roger's partner in his law firm was pressing them to set the date for their wedding because didn't she know overseas clients needed at least six months' notice, maybe more? And, most important of all, Roger's golf handicap had come down to ten.

He'd talked for close on an hour so he must have said more than that, but for the life of her Bryony couldn't remember what.

She'd spent the rest of Sunday deciding—and deciding again—and deciding again—what to wear and what to take to Melbourne. Twin set or tweeds… She didn't possess either. She knew how to be conservative, though, and, when Jack and Maddy collected her on Monday, Maddy's face fell in disappointment.

'I didn't think you wore black clothes.'

'Black and white.' Maddy had raced up the path before Jack, and Bryony had scooped her up into her arms to hug her. 'White blouse. Black pants. City business clothes. We're going to the city on business.'

'Does that mean we can't have fun?'

Bryony grinned. 'I have a red skirt in my suitcase,' she confided.

And then Jack was there, and the look on his face said he was disappointed, too. They hadn't wanted a professional interior designer, Bryony thought; they'd wanted a

84

partner in escapism. It couldn't be helped, she decided firmly. With the way Jack Morgan made her feel, if she wore her harem pants, her engagement wouldn't be worth a sausage by the end of the day.

Her engagement was important, she'd decided. Roger was her future. He was her secure, trusting friend, he'd done nothing to deserve disloyalty, and Jack Morgan wasn't any woman's future. Except maybe Diana's. So she resisted the impulse to bolt back to her bedroom and change into something brighter.

'Isn't Harry coming?' Maddy asked, and as Bryony told her Harry was staying with Myrna her face fell still further.

'Jack says Jessie has to stay home, too. Are you sure you've packed a red skirt?'

'Promise.' She set Maddy down on her feet again and smoothed the creases in her suit before greeting Jack. They met each other politely—business acquaintances—and passed trite comments on the weather as she supervised the loading of her suitcase into Jack's car.

Some car! Bryony's eyes widened when she saw it. It was a Peugeot, wide, sleek, fast. Expensive. Lovely leather seats that folded around her. Maddy sat on a booster seat in the back and Bryony stretched her legs out in the passenger seat and felt like a cat. A sleek, well-cared-for cat.

'You like my car, then?'

Bryony looked across to find Jack watching her, as if he was bemused. Jack *was* bemused. This lady was the most sensual woman he'd ever known. If something felt good, then she loved it. She was like a cat...

Bryony's eyes widened even further as she saw his expression change, and guessed what he was thinking. Drat the man. He saw too much. She smoothed imaginary creases from her trousers again and folded her hands primly on her lap.

'It's a very nice car,' she said demurely.

'Beats the truck?'

He was laughing at her and there was a challenge in his voice.

'Yes.' She glared at him and he laughed out loud.

'I'm sorry. It's just...you change to fit your circumstances. You sat in my work truck when Maddy and I brought you and Harry home from the show and you looked like you were meant to be there, dung and all. Now... You look incredibly different. Like you belong in a Peugeot.'

'Well, you do, too,' Bryony retorted, slightly breathless.

It was true. Jack had replaced his moleskins and work shirts with smart casual trousers and a soft linen open-necked shirt that screamed quality. His black curls were gleaming in the sunlight streaming in from the opened sun-roof and his dark eyes reflected his pleasure in the day.

'Okay, then.' He smiled, then his smile slipped a little as he glanced back at Maddy sitting self-consciously in her booster seat. 'The only one not dressed for the city is our Maddy. I can't persuade her to wear anything but her dun-garees.'

'Grandma bought me these dungarees.' Maddy's voice was dangerous, loaded. The dungarees were important. They were definitely worn, though, Bryony thought. Any minute now those seams might burst.

'Maddy, it'd be a shame if you wore out Grandma's dun-garees by wearing them every day,' Bryony said thoughtfully. 'What say we make our first port of call a shop I know in Carlton? I know the lady who owns it and Jodie has the most beautiful clothes...'

'I like my dungarees.'

Bryony considered, and sighed. She knew she could help here—but it meant dispensing with her armour, dispensing with her business suit.

'Tell you what,' Bryony said, throwing caution to the wind. 'You don't like my suit, right?'

'No.' Maddy was definite. 'I don't. Apart from your lovely hair, you look like Diana in that suit.'

Perish the thought! Maybe this idea wasn't so bad after all.

'Well, Jodie—my friend in Carlton—makes clothes for all ages and I think they're fabulous.' Bryony chuckled. 'Let's say we both shock Jack's socks off and buy two splendid going-to-the-city-to-have-fun outfits. One for me and one for you.'

'But my dungarees...'

'If Jodie has something you'd like to wear, we'll wrap your dungarees in red tissue paper, tie them with ribbon and carry them carefully home with us so they won't get damaged in the city,' Bryony promised. 'How does that sound?'

Maddy considered carefully.

'Does Jodie sell black and white clothes like you're wearing now?'

'I don't think she's ever heard of black and white. Her favourite colour is tangerine.'

'What's tangerine?'

'Wait and see. If you want to, that is.'

Maddy made her decision. 'I think I want to.'

Bryony smiled—and turned to find Jack watching her with an expression on his face she'd caught a couple of times before—as if she'd just stepped off a flying saucer.

What followed was a very busy, very happy day.

First a trip to Jodie's. Jodie was a friend from way back to childhood. She greeted Bryony with joy, Maddy with friendship and adult respect—and Jack with blatant curiosity. She spent the whole time they were in the shop trying to get Bryony alone for an inquisition, but Bryony wasn't having a bar of it. Neither was Jack.

Bryony had suggested he find himself a coffee while the girls shopped, but he refused to leave and spent the time browsing through the shop, producing one outrageous outfit after another, and not just for Maddy.

Jack's little daughter came out of the dressing room, shy

and self-conscious in bright red trousers and a matching red and white blouse—ready to bolt back to her dungarees any minute—to find Jack holding up an impossibly tiny black and silver dress, cut almost to the waist at the neckline and almost to the waist at the hem.

'Bryony, this is *you*,' Jack said gravely.

Maddy gasped and Bryony choked.

'You *have* to be joking!' Bryony turned to Maddy. 'Your Jack is trying to get me arrested,' she told Maddy. She grinned at the avidly interested saleswoman. 'Jodie, what are you doing selling dresses like *this*? No respectable woman on this earth could wear that dress.'

'You'd be surprised,' Jodie told her, matching her grin. 'I made the first one as a one-off for a very sexy client, but now I sell heaps of them. Mostly to women on the wrong side of forty and on the outside of too many sticky date puddings. Their husbands love them.'

'I'd love this,' Jack announced, and Bryony glared.

'Just lucky you're not my husband, then.'

'Roger would love this.'

'Roger would send me home to change.'

He would, too. Roger would approve of the neat black and white business suit she was wearing. Roger would have a pink fit at the dress Jack was holding up. It did look…fun! Oh, dear…

'It'd look great on you,' Jodie told her. 'It needs someone with your figure to carry it off.'

'I'd be more respectable in a bikini.'

'It sparkles,' Maddy said wistfully. 'You could just wear it tonight when Roger won't see you. For us…'

The three of them were looking at her with eyes holding various expressions. Jack's was challenging and mocking. Jodie's was bug-eyed and laughing. Maddy's was just plain yearning.

It was the yearning that got to her. Maddy was yearning to have some fun. Life had tossed this little girl around. There hadn't been too much fun—ever. In a few months

Bryony would be a lawyer's wife, Roger's wife. Ditto for Bryony for the future.

She caught herself up. *Bryony—stop thinking like this! This minute! Change the subject, fast.*

'What do you think of the clothes you have on, Maddy?' Bryony asked, and Maddy looked down. With the attention mostly diverted from her small person by the outlandish dress Jack was holding, the child could consider without being pressured.

'They're neat,' she conceded. 'Pretty.'

The saleswoman agreed. 'They look great. And I have a heap of bright red ribbon in the back room,' Jodie told her. 'We could let out your plaits, tie your hair loosely back with the ribbon and let your curls hang free like Bryony's.'

'Like Bryony's'. Magic words.

'My hair's not like Bryony's,' Maddy said sadly, fingering her plaits. She obviously did them herself. They were dragged together, one forward from her ear and the other back. Bryony knew without being told that no one was allowed to help this child dress.

'It is like Bryony's, you know,' Jodie said definitely. 'I can see curls popping out all over. Do you know, I knew Bryony when she was seven years old and she wore plaits just like yours? She looked like you, too—only her face was always dirtier and her clothes were torn. Bryony couldn't even make it from her place to church on Sundays without tearing her clothes. Bryony's hair is bright red and yours is a gorgeous blonde, but otherwise you're a pigeon pair.'

'Really?' Maddy was almost dumbfounded by the suggestion.

'Really.'

'Jodie, do you have a sparkly party dress for Maddy, too?' Jack demanded, still holding Bryony's handkerchief dress as if loath to let it go. 'Something to make tonight really festive?'

'I sure do.' Jodie held out her hand to Maddy. 'Come and see. Would you like to buy a party dress?'

Maddy tilted her chin.

'Only if Bryony buys that one.'

'Maddy, I can't afford it,' Bryony wailed. She knew expensive when she saw it.

'No sweat.' Jack's eyes gleamed pure mischief. 'This one's on me. My wedding present to Roger.'

'You're kidding. It's not respectable enough.'

'Bryony Lester, the last time you were respectable was before I was born,' Jodie said darkly. 'Since when have things changed?'

They hadn't.

Bryony stood in front of her bedroom mirror at the hotel that night and eyed herself in dismay. The dress left nothing to the imagination at all. It covered her—just. She wore slinky black stockings and high heels. The tiny black and silver dress—or waist wrap—made her *just* respectable, but somewhere Bryony's great-aunt Bertha was turning in her grave.

'That girl will come to no good,' she'd told Bryony's mother over and over again, and Bryony wrinkled her nose into the mirror at the long-gone Aunt Bertha.

'Well, now you've finally been proved right, Aunty B. It's just as well I didn't let him pay for the thing because that would have been the last straw. Strange men buying me dresses like this... All I need now is to buy a flashing red lamp for my door...'

She looked down at the child by her side.

'Maddy, I just know this dress is going to get me into trouble.'

Maddy tucked her hand into Bryony's and gave her a reassuring grin.

'No, it won't. We're just going to tea with Jack. He'll look after us.'

Hmm. Faith like this was unanswerable but Bryony

looked down at Maddy and she couldn't think of a thing
to say. The more Maddy was learning to trust her father,
the more Bryony wasn't. His eyes were dangerous. The
whole man was dangerous.

Bryony and Maddy were sharing a room. The adjoining
door went through to Jack's room and they could hear him
whistling while he dressed.

'Do you think Jack really likes my dress?' Maddy asked
shyly, and Bryony stooped so they were the same eye level
in the mirror. Stooping was hard. She checked her cleavage
to make sure nothing had popped right out. It was
okay—just! She held Maddy round the waist and hugged
her.

'Jack loves you and he sure does love your dress, Maddy.
The moment he saw it he loved it and you're making him
as proud as a peacock by wearing it.' Maddy's frock was
the colour of rainbows, and was made of frills, frills and
more frills. It was way over the top—the sort of dress every
little girl dreamed of owning. Jodie had supplied white and
gold ribbons for her hair, and the tiny Maddy looked like
something from the top of a Christmas tree.

Maddy had stared at it open-mouthed when Jodie had
produced it. She hadn't said a word, but her eyes had said
it all. Just once in every little girl's life she should own a
dress like this. But Bryony shouldn't look like *this*!

The whistling next door stopped. There was a knock on
the door. Bryony took a last panicking glance at the mirror
as she straightened. Carefully. Good grief! She was all legs
and breasts with a tiny bit of sparkle in between. She hauled
her hair around her shoulders in a futile attempt to hide
some cleavage. It didn't help one bit, and Maddy was tugging her hand.

'Jack's waiting for us. Come on, Bryony.'

All Bryony wanted to do was dive under the bedclothes
and stay there. She was operating way out of her control—and she knew it.

Then they opened the door—and Jack's eyes saw Bryony—and the world tilted even further on its axis.

It didn't stop tilting.

The Grand Dining Room at the Windsor was magic— vast and wonderful. The food looked fabulous. Jack in a dinner suit was a man who made heads turn.

It seemed every head in the room turned to stare at the three of them as they entered. At Jack. At Maddy. And at the woman in the tiny dress—all black and silver and fiery red curls!

People smiled as they passed. Bryony could read their thoughts. A lovely couple with their lovely daughter... Their clothes and their body language said they were here for a truly special occasion, as Bryony told Jack and Maddy.

'Which we are,' Jack announced after they'd been seated, and he was pouring champagne into three glasses. 'Maddy, I know it's against the law for six-year-olds to drink alcohol and after the first sip it's back to lemonade for you, but it's a champagne toast first. Today I've spent more money and had more fun than I have in years.'

They all had. Bryony had spent Jack's money as if it was going out of fashion. She and Maddy had chosen the most wonderful furnishings for a child's bedroom that any little girl could dream of, and Jack had stood back and watched them like a benevolent and benign genie.

They'd caused an economic boom in Melbourne all by themselves today, Bryony thought, but Maddy was glowing with happiness and it was worth every cent they'd paid.

'Here's to your bedroom!' Jack raised his glass. 'There's only the ship's chest left to find and then we're finished.'

'Jack...' Maddy said her father's name tentatively and her voice wobbled.

Jack smiled down at his daughter and his smile made Bryony's heart turn over. This wasn't a mischief or a wickedness or a seduction smile. This was a man who loved his little daughter so much it hurt.

'Maddy?'

'I've been thinking about the chest Bryony said we could find. The chest to pack my clothes in so I can take them away again…'

'Mmm?' Jack's murmur was non-committal. The world held its breath.

'I think…' Maddy held her champagne glass and turned it around and around in her fingers. A child about to make an important announcement… 'If it's okay…' She took a deep breath. 'At Grandma's I had a great big wooden chest of drawers.'

'You'd like one like that instead of a ship's chest?' Jack's voice was infinitely gentle and Bryony scarcely dared breathe.

'I think…' Maddy's elfin face grew even paler. 'Well, my grandma's dead and my mom doesn't want me. Will you…? Will you keep on wanting me?'

Will you keep on wanting me…? It was a cry from the heart, and it was all Bryony could do not to burst into tears. Jack closed his eyes, and Bryony saw the pain. Then he opened them again.

'I've always wanted you, Maddy,' Jack said steadily, and he reached across the table and took the child's face between his large, capable hands. 'I've always wanted you and I always will. You're my daughter. Now and for ever.'

Maddy nodded, and swallowed.

'And…and can I call you Daddy? Like…like Fiona calls her daddy?'

'You sure can, sweetheart.' Then Jack looked over at Bryony and grinned. 'You sure can. There's nothing I'd like better. But we have a problem here, Maddy. Miss Lester, can I lend you a handkerchief?'

'Yes,' Bryony said desperately. 'Unless you want me to blow my nose on a table napkin. You go and enact me a scene like this and I haven't even got a tissue—because there's nowhere in this ridiculous dress to hide anything bigger than a postage stamp. Quick!' She retired behind her hand and waved her spare fingers desperately at Jack.

Jack's grin broadened. He placed a man-sized handkerchief in her fingers and Bryony blew, hard, and then tried to hand it back again. 'No, no. You keep it!'

'So where will I put it?' Bryony asked, her voice strained to breaking. She emerged from behind her hand, waterlogged but recovered enough to glare. 'Where, Jack Morgan...?'

He took the handkerchief back and chuckled. Then he raised his glass and waited until his daughter and Bryony had raised theirs.

'Here's to a wonderful day,' he said softly. 'To two wonderful ladies, and to being Maddy's daddy.'

They all drank to that.

After the meal there was dancing. Maddy was dead tired but when the first couple moved onto the dance floor her eyes lit like candles.

'I can dance,' she said urgently. 'I can. And this is a dancing dress.'

It was, too. If anything was a dancing dress, Maddy's dress was.

'You're on.' Jack was on his feet in a flash, holding his hands out to his daughter. 'If you'll excuse us, Miss Lester...'

A minute later they were spinning around the dance floor while Bryony watched in amazement. The child was a natural born dancer—and so was Jack. She should have known. Jack's wife—Maddy's mother—had been an internationally renowned ballet dancer. Georgia would never have married a man who couldn't dance. And Maddy... Jack's hands held her tiny form before him, guiding her lightly in a waltz, and Maddy moved with intuition and grace.

Jack had taken his handkerchief back!

Bryony sat and played with her wine and wondered how

on earth she could get rid of this lump in her throat. She just had to look at the pair of them and she'd cry… What was happening to her? She'd never felt like this. Never! As if, if she left for Sydney tomorrow and never saw this man and his daughter again, she'd break her heart! Then they were spinning back to her as the waltz came to an end and Bryony swallowed and forced a smile.

'It's your turn, Bryony,' Maddy said urgently. 'You've got a dance dress on, too.'

'I don't think so. If I jiggle in this dress I might jiggle straight out!'

'But I want to finish my lemonade and watch you.' Maddy flopped into her chair and fixed her father with a look. 'Make her, Daddy!'

The band started playing a tango. A tango! For heaven's sake… Jack was looking down at her with those eyes that were so dangerous she should run a mile. Or maybe a thousand. Maybe all the way to Roger.

'Your dress is far too beautiful to waste by hiding half of it under a table for the entire night,' Jack told her. 'Come and air it.'

'Half of it isn't hidden under the table,' Bryony said desperately. 'It doesn't exist! And it doesn't need airing. This is the most ventilating dress I've ever worn in my life.'

'You know, of all the adjectives I can think of to describe your dress, ventilating isn't one of them.' Jack took her hand and pulled her to her feet, brooking no opposition. 'Miss Lester, they're playing a tango. Can I teach you the steps?'

'It's quite easy,' Maddy said helpfully between mouthfuls of lemonade. 'Grandma showed me.'

'Thank you both,' Bryony retorted, with dignity. 'But I know how to tango.'

'Did Roger teach you?'

Bryony stiffened. There was a load of polite scepticism in Jack's voice.

'Roger's a fine dancer.'

He was. He took his dancing very seriously, did Roger, never missing a step and concentrating absolutely on the movements. Boring but fine.

'Well, bully for Roger.' Jack pulled her tight against him, holding her by the waist as he led her firmly out to the dance floor. 'Let's see how I compare.'

There was no comparison. No comparison at all. Bryony had been in Jack's arms for no longer than twenty seconds before she stopped even trying to think about Roger. Or think about anything but how it felt to be held by Jack Morgan.

This man was *some* farmer! He danced as if he'd been born on the dance floor, his movements more intuitive and fluid than Roger's could ever be after a lifetime of dancing lessons. He held her against him, firmly but naturally, almost as an extension of himself, then absorbed the music into his body and let the dance happen around them.

All the time his eyes held hers, laughing and vibrant. There was no concentration on the dance's complex movements. There was only concentration on the girl in his arms, as though the skills of the demanding tango were absolutely secondary to enjoyment, to ensuring that Bryony was enjoying herself.

She was. In those twenty seconds it took to have him hold her against him and move onto the dance floor in the first few complex steps, Bryony's ridiculous dress was forgotten, the diners around the dance floor were forgotten— even Maddy, watching them big-eyed from behind her lemonade. There was only the feel of this man's arms holding her, pulling her, twisting her out and then reeling her back to him. The beat of the music in her brain and the heat from her body and the feel of Jack's strength and sheer, wonderful maleness against her was all that mattered.

The heat... The fire... Jack.

They were alone on the dance floor now. The tango was a demanding, riveting dance and others had abandoned it.

Bryony and Jack, moving together—her slim, lovely form moving with grace in his arms, his dark and consummate good looks in his jet-black dinner suit—were a sight to make the whole dining room cease eating, cease talking, and simply stare.

But Bryony was oblivious. She was in Jack's arms. Somewhere around the second turn of the dance floor it hit her with blinding clarity—the one conscious thought that she was capable of. It was hardly a thought; it was simply an extension of herself. The fact had been like a bud, dormant and waiting in the wings to reveal itself, and now it unfurled, blossomed and swelled until it threatened to consume her.

There was nothing she could do to prevent it happening. It was the overwhelming consciousness that she was where she wanted to be for the rest of her life. That life couldn't get any better than it was at this moment. That she was head over heels in love with Jack Morgan.

CHAPTER SEVEN

THE dance had to end. It always did end, some time. The music slowed, and slowed some more, and the lovely haze deepened. Bryony moved into Jack in the last sweet movement and clung—and then the music died completely and there was the sound of clapping around them and somehow—somehow—Bryony had to make her feet touch earth again.

Jack was caressing her hair very gently with his lips.

'You're right,' he said in a voice that was none too steady and was meant just for her. 'You *can* tango.'

She gave a half-hearted chuckle and turned within the confines of Jack's arms to see Maddy clapping with the rest of the diners. Goodness—everyone was watching! She tried a smile and Jack took her hand firmly in his—possessively—and led her back to the table.

'That was the best tango I've ever seen,' Maddy said eagerly, regarding them with awe as they came back to her. 'Even on the dancing videos Grandma showed me. You were just beautiful.' She sighed. 'And just at the end the waitress brought me another lemonade, and you know what she said? She said I was a lucky girl to have you for a mummy and a daddy because it was lovely to see people who loved each other so much.'

She paused for breath. So did Bryony. She stopped breathing entirely. But Maddy hadn't finished.

'I liked her thinking I have a mummy and a daddy who love each other,' she confided. 'It feels special.' She looked from Jack to Bryony and back again to her father. 'Is she right? Do you love each other?'

Bryony blushed—from the tips of her toes to the roots

of her fiery hair. Then Jack was lifting Maddy high into his arms and smiling down at her, breaking the moment.

'The tango's the dance of lovers,' he told his daughter. 'When you dance the tango you have to forget everything else—just be in love with the lady you're dancing with.'

'You mean...you mean you were pretending? You don't love Bryony?'

'I wouldn't quite say that.' Jack's smile was strained and he changed the subject fast. 'Maddy, you must be exhausted. I think it's time we took you up to bed. Right, Miss Lester?'

Miss Lester...

The heat had faded. Bryony gave an involuntary shiver. 'Yes.' She hugged her arms beneath her breasts, trying to keep the cold at bay in the beautifully heated room. 'Let's go.'

Maddy was so close to sleep, she hardly made it to bed.

They undressed her, cleaned her teeth and tucked her into the twin bed beside Bryony's. Bryony started to tell her the *Harry the Dirty Dog* story, but Maddy was asleep before she'd remembered three lines.

Maddy drifted off with a smile curving her lips. For one small girl, it had been a truly wonderful day.

Bryony's voice died away to nothing. She faltered to a halt, then looked up to find Jack watching. She'd sat on Maddy's bed while she'd started the story, but Jack was standing at the door, his arms folded. Watching.

'It's only nine o'clock,' he told her, his eyes thoughtful, almost wary. 'What say we watch a movie in my room?'

That seemed dangerous. She certainly wasn't dressed for an evening alone with Jack Morgan. Bryony looked doubtfully down at her dress. All she could see from her angle was cleavage. She didn't want to go to bed, but to go next door was surely crazy...

'Not in this dress,' she said at last, decisively.

'Why not in that dress?'

'Because I'm engaged to Roger.'

He smiled but Bryony's uncertainty was reflected in his eyes. Maybe he was feeling the same way. That things were liable to get right out of hand here. Fast.

'So you'll put your business suit back on?'

'No.' She managed a smile as well. 'I have a jogging suit in my bag.'

'In case you want to jog?'

'I might,' she said with dignity. 'Sometimes I get up at dawn and jog.'

'Yeah?'

'Once I did,' she told him. 'Back in 1995. June the fourteenth. Five thirty-seven a.m., to be precise. I jogged until five fifty-eight.'

His mouth curved. 'Not habit-forming, then?'

'It might have been. I had an appointment with my pillow the next morning so I never found out. But you never know when the urge to jog will strike again,' Bryony told him. 'I'm a girl who likes to be prepared. And see—I was right. A jogging suit is just the thing to watch movies in.'

Jack appeared to consider. 'You don't think it could be a tad formal for two people sharing a family suite? I thought we might just watch a movie in our pyjamas.'

She rolled her eyes. 'Yeah, right...'

In your dreams, buster!

'Okay.' The irrepressible grin took over and he held up two hands in defeat. 'I'll go check the movie channel and do some choosing. You go get into your chastity suit or whatever...'

'Jack...'

'I know.' He kept his hands high and sighed. 'You trust yourself entirely. You only have to think of your Roger and you go weak at the knees with passion and absolute, unswerving devotion. It's only me you don't trust.' He gave her another smile—a smile that really did make her go weak at the knees—and left her to it.

*   *   *

There was champagne in an ice bucket on the table.

Bryony saw it as soon as she stepped through the adjoining door and she darn near backed out again. She'd drunk one glass of champagne and one glass of wine all night, but that was quite enough. She was already feeling dizzy.

'Very nice!' Jack's eyes ran approvingly over Bryony's slim form. He'd hauled off his jacket and tie and loosened his collar but Bryony had changed completely. She was now clad from neck to toe in a crimson jogging suit. 'Very demure. Pity about the colour!'

'What's wrong with the colour?'

'It's red. With your hair…well, you're all red.'

'Red's my favourite colour.'

'I guessed that.' He shook his head. 'I don't know, though, Miss Lester. The headmistress at my old school wouldn't let the girls wear red to the school dances. She said it was a colour that ignites passion.'

Passion…

Bryony took a deep breath. *Keep it light.*

'Yeah?' She managed a grin and flopped down on the settee beside him. 'Well, I left my patent leather shoes off, if that's any consolation.'

'Patent leather shoes…?'

'That's another thing we weren't allowed to wear to school dances. They're shiny and they reflect your knickers.'

Bryony shook her head and reached for a chocolate. They'd magically appeared on the table with the champagne. 'There's nothing you need to tell me about you men.' She sighed in despondent reflection. 'Miss Morrison told us the horrid facts when we were wide-eyed and innocent and twelve years old. We thought guys just liked looking at our nice, shiny shoes and all the time you were staring down trying to see a bit of reflected cottontail.'

'Cottontail?'

Bryony glared. 'If you don't know what cottontails are, then use your imagination.'

'I just did.' Jack laughed, his eyes creasing into deep channels the way Bryony loved them to crease, and he poured them both champagne. 'Cottontails... Well, well...' Then he took pity on Bryony and the mischief eased. 'You have the choice of movie, Miss Lester.'

'Yeah?'

Another chocolate went the way of the first. Nerves. When in doubt, eat!

'We have *The Fearless Vampire Killers*, *An Officer and a Gentleman* or *Bugs Bunny*.'

'No contest,' Bryony said definitely. '*An Officer and A Gentleman*.'

His eyebrows went right up. 'I sort of thought *Fearless Vampire Killers*...'

'Does *Fearless Vampire Killers* have Richard Gere as hero?'

'No, but...'

'But what?' She eyed him cautiously. 'Are you saying vampires can compete with *my* Richard?'

'*Your* Richard...?'

'I fell in love with Richard Gere in *Pretty Woman*,' she explained. 'You know the bit where Julia Roberts goes under the bubbles? I keep fantasising it's me who pops up instead of her. He makes my toes curl. So if we're watching movies together just sit down, shut up, move the chocolates closer and watch my toes curl.'

Jack did just that. And so did Bryony's toes. By the time the movie ended, her toes were so curled she thought she'd never get them straight, but she wasn't the least bit sure if the cause was Richard Gere.

Sure, Richard was impossibly handsome as the young lieutenant, swinging his lady into his arms and carrying her off into a mist of happy-ever-after. But there was also the champagne and the wonderful chocolates...

There was also Jack, sitting beside her, watching the movie, watching her. She'd concentrated on the movie really hard, all the time, but for once Richard Gere hadn't stood a chance. He was good-looking all right, but so was Jack Morgan... Whew! There were tiny prickles of heat running up and down her spine. The jogging suit she was wearing was far too hot.

Her birthday suit would have been too hot at this moment!

The credits rolled and she made herself get off the settee, standing up on feet that were none too steady. She wobbled. She definitely wobbled. Jack rose swiftly beside her and took her arms in his big hands.

'Whoa... How much champagne have you had?'

'Three glasses,' she said with dignity. 'I'm not drunk. And I'm not planning on driving.'

She just had to get through the door at the other side of the room. She didn't want to. She wanted to stay right where she was, being held by Jack. What did a lady do when she didn't want to move from where she was? Wobble some more?

She leaned back and let Jack take her weight.

'Bryony...'

'I'm not drunk,' she repeated. 'Three champagnes in four hours is hardly drunk territory.'

'Maybe you'd better go to bed.'

His voice sounded strained. Bed. That sounded a really wonderful idea. There was a vast bed right behind them. Vast!

Jack had booked them a family suite. One big bed in one room for the mummy and the daddy, and one room with twin beds for the kids.

Now Bryony had to go back to the kids' room, and dream of Roger, while Jack Morgan slept in his big bed alone, dreaming of Diana... Dear heaven... Bryony was hurtling down a path with the speed of light, and she'd never even known the path existed until this minute.

'Jack...'

'Do you want me to carry you?'

Oh, help! He really did think she was drunk. A girl had to have some dignity. She hauled herself back from him and stood erect, not a wobble in sight.

'No.'

She tilted her chin and looked at him. He looked at her. Mistake. Big mistake. On a scale of one to ten, that look had to rate about a hundred and twelve! Because all of a sudden it was unbearable. Unbearable that he should stand there with his top shirt buttons undone and the hairs of his chest actually showing and his sleeves rolled up and his arms all brown from the sun.

And that irresistible little smile playing at the corners of his mouth.

It was unbearable that she should stand a good twelve inches away and there was air—actual air!—between them. Anything between them was unbearable. An inch would be too much...

Afterwards Bryony could never remember who moved first—whether she took the first step or he did—but all of a sudden the air disappeared with a whoosh. She was in his arms.

He was crushing her against him with a longing and a passion that had absolutely nothing to do with Bryony's engagement to Roger or Jack's good, sensible decisions about Diana, or anything at all in the outside world—or anything in the entire universe.

Only a man and a woman and their absolute need. Their need for each other. She needed him. She needed him like life itself. Dear heaven, he was her home. He was...

Jack's arms held hers, fierce and possessive—triumphant—and Bryony melted into him as if she could never get close enough. Her face turned up to his, desperate to find his mouth, then her lips were beneath his. Her mouth

was open—wanting—demanding—searching to know this
man as she'd never known anyone in her life before.

This man was her soul; she could feel it. He smiled at
her and his smile reached her heart. He laughed at her and
his laugh was a caress all in itself. He held his little daughter with love and pride, and Bryony's heart turned over
within her. He twisted her heart in two.

And now... Now he was making her body wild with a
desire she'd never known in her life before. He set her on
fire. All she could feel was the wanting and the heat throb-
bing through every vein in her body. Her hands came
around to haul him in closer and she could feel the heat of
his body through the fine fabric of his shirt.

'Jack...Jack...'

Heaven knew how she said his name—or even *if* she did.
Her whole body was dissolving in a mist of love and light
and desire and all she wanted was to be a part of him. And
he wanted her.

His hands were under her jogging top, searching beneath
the fine lace contours of her bra. She felt his strong, wide
fingers knead against the smooth curves of each breast, and
she felt the magic response of each nipple in turn.

Her nipples knew what they wanted. They wanted this
man to touch them. They wanted... They wanted what she
wanted. To be closer... Closer...

Then, somehow, her jogging top was being lifted from
her. Her bra was disappearing to the floor and then they
were both falling backwards onto the magnificent luxury of
the bed. The bed enfolded them, caressed them all by itself
and the fire intensified.

Jack was moving down from above her, kissing each
breast, his tongue stroking the smooth skin until she felt
that she'd scream with joy and love. His hands were cup-
ping her thighs and pulling her up to him in a fiercely
possessive act of love, and she could feel the matching
arousal of his loins.

He wanted her as much as she wanted him. Bryony caught his dark curls and tangled her fingers in their midst, arching her breasts against his wonderful, magic mouth.

Then she slid her hands down—down—down beneath the waistband of his trousers... Damn... The things were far too tight. Somehow she twisted her hands in between their clinging bodies to undo the buckle of his belt and then, as she was there anyway—well, why not?—she slid her hands even further until she felt what she wanted against her—within her—so badly, she thought she'd die of wanting...

'Jack...'

The zip slid down, and the tiny movement stopped him, like the click of the trigger of a gun. He pulled back, arching above her, looking down with eyes that were blank with shock and desire and wonder—all three emotions rolled into one. Somehow he made his mouth move, and when he spoke his voice was jagged with desire.

'Bryony... I'm not... I can't...'

She knew. She knew. With a tiny triumphant groan she rolled from the bed. Men! No forethought at all!

'Stay,' she ordered, with the same hopefulness she tried with Harry, and somehow she managed to get out of the room and into the one she was sharing with Maddy. It was lucky Maddy was so tired bombs wouldn't wake her. What she'd think if she saw Bryony like this...

Where had she put it? Where...? Fumbling fingers in her toilet bag... She *did* have one. Then she was back next door and he'd stayed—gee, Harry never did that!—and she was ripping the foil from the tiny package and handing it to her love...

'I told you, I'm a girl who likes to be prepared.'

It was said lightly, teasingly, but the blank look in Jack's eyes had changed in the minute she'd been gone. A minute ago it had been shock and love and desire. Now... Now it was just shock.

He dropped back onto the bedcovers and looked up at her, and the jagged edge to his voice had changed too.

'You brought a condom...'

Dear heaven, she knew the voice. It was an accusation!

'I...' All of a sudden Bryony was unsure, really unsure. She felt like a kid who'd been kicked in the teeth when she'd been expecting to be hugged. Like a woman who'd been kicked instead of kissed. She must be wrong. It mustn't be an accusation. This was crazy! So take up where she'd left off?

She stooped and kissed Jack on the mouth—long and lingering—but she wasn't wrong. Now it was definitely different. Horribly different.

Jack didn't respond at all. His hands didn't move to touch her and his mouth stayed closed, as though he wondered what on earth she was doing. He was suddenly rigidly—dreadfully—under control.

She stopped kissing him and stood up. Dignity. She needed dignity here. Fast! Her chin tilted, and she grabbed her jogging top and held it against her chest. She wasn't ready to be labelled a scarlet woman.

'You planned this!' His voice was flat now, accusatory.

Bryony closed her eyes.

The night had turned to nightmare.

'I didn't plan...'

'You brought condoms.'

'I carry them in my cosmetics bag.' She took a deep breath, but there was no getting away from the rejection in his voice.

'Do you always carry condoms, then—just in case you jump into bed with the next man you meet? Or did you plan this particularly for me?'

There was fury in his voice. Sheer, plain fury, as if he'd caught her setting a trap... A trap... If he thought she'd set this up—was trying to seduce him, for heaven's sake!— then there was only one thing to do. Get out of here fast.

She held up the fingers of her left hand, and the diamond Roger had given her sparkled in the light.

'I'm engaged to be married and I'm not ready for babies,' she said in a voice that trembled so much it was hardly audible. There were tears behind her voice but he mustn't know that. 'So I carry condoms. I didn't bring them here deliberately.'

The fury mounted. Jack's face was as cold as a slab of ice.

'How can you flash some man's ring at me and throw me a condom?'

Unanswerable. She couldn't even answer herself on that one. All she could do was get away from him. Quick.

'I don't know,' she told him, and somehow she found the courage to put an edge of anger in her voice. How dared he make her feel like this? Like a tramp! 'I don't... I don't feel engaged when you're with me and that's the truth. But you obviously think we're crazy and maybe you're right. So it must have been the champagne. I must have been drunk after all. Because there's no way in the wide world I would have wanted to kiss you otherwise, Jack Morgan. No way at all.'

As an exit line it was a beauty. It got her all the way back into the other room with the bolt slid home before she burst into tears. Then she washed her face fifteen or so times, retired under the bedclothes, and burned with humiliation.

Look before you leap. How many times had that line been drilled into her by her parents and teachers and friends? Bryony Lester, who always acted on impulse, who wore her heart on her sleeve, who tumbled through life with joy.

Well, life had slapped her back into place now. This was worse even than when she'd dived into the swimming hole at the end of summer without checking the depth and darn near broke her neck. A back brace for three months was nothing to this. She was way out of line, and she knew it.

Dear heaven, where did she go from here?

CHAPTER EIGHT

BRYONY spent the next week trying to work, trying to be sensible and practical and not so mortified she couldn't think straight, and trying to stay engaged to Roger.

She couldn't. She knew, in her heart, what she had to do. On the following Saturday she left a heap of dog food for Harry—she didn't want to tell Myrna or anyone else where she was going and why—and caught a plane for Sydney. When she came back on Sunday night she wasn't wearing an engagement ring.

Amazingly, Roger had seemed more annoyed than upset. But he had been *very* annoyed.

'Bryony, you realise we've booked the best restaurant in Sydney for our reception and I've asked people already. How can you do this? If this is one of your scatter-brained ideas...'

Then he'd got around to threats.

'Bryony, I need to be married. If you don't marry me now, then I'm going to have to find someone else.'

He would, too, Bryony had realised, and with six months to go before the restaurant booking he had time to do it.

Despite Roger's annoyance, they'd had a lovely dinner together on the Saturday night—and by the time Bryony had left him on Sunday she could already see the cogs whirring as to who would be suitable as Bryony's replacement.

It wasn't that he was devoted to her absolutely. It was just that she'd suited him and he'd never bothered thinking of alternatives. He was the same as she'd been up until now, and she hoped he didn't get any lightning bolts thundering into his love life in the future to disrupt his comfortable plans.

Or maybe she hoped he did. She liked Roger. He wore lovely suits and it'd be great if he found a lightning bolt who wanted him.

She'd found her lightning bolt, but he didn't want her. But at least she knew what a lightning bolt was now. So she'd kissed Roger goodbye and wished him well and, when she'd climbed on her aeroplane bound back to Hamilton, Bryony had never felt so lonely in her life before.

On Wednesday the furnishings arrived for Maddy's room.

Everything. They looked wonderful—just as wonderful as they had in Melbourne when they'd chosen them. Myrna came round and she and Bryony had fun cutting and sewing the silk drapes and the curtains. It was a real pleasure to work with good-quality fabric, and both of them knew how much Maddy would love it.

Half the pleasure for Bryony was that when they finished she would get to deliver it. Pleasure... Or dread?

A mix of both. But it was better than sitting at home and not seeing either Maddy or Jack. She'd go on the following Saturday, Bryony thought. They'd have everything made by then, and Maddy would be home from school.

'You want me to ring and make you an appointment?' Myrna asked. She was troubled. Bryony might think she was cheerful, but Myrna had never seen her friend so quiet.

'No.'

Myrna wrinkled her nose and tried not to look at the white circle on Bryony's hand where Roger's ring had been. If Bryony didn't want to tell her, then Myrna wouldn't ask, but it was nearly killing her not to.

'Why not?'

'Because Jack might just come and pick them up himself and I want to see Maddy, and Harry wants to see Jess. Harry loves Jessica.'

It was too much. Myrna couldn't keep her mouth shut any longer.

'And you love Jack?'

'Myrna...'

'I know.' Myrna held up her hands. 'It's none of my business. It's just... Bryony, I wish you all the luck in the world.'

'Well, I'm going to need it,' Bryony muttered. 'He thinks I'm a flibbertigibbet.'

'Yeah?' Myrna grinned. 'He couldn't be right there, could he?'

'Yeah, well...'

Bryony's face fell and Myrna's grin died. She moved forward to give her a swift hug. Oh, dear.

'You'll just have to teach him to love flibbertigibbets,' she said solidly. 'I do.'

'You don't think I could change? Learn to wear pearls and read a recipe book and—'

'Bryony!' Myrna shook her head. 'Hey, that's the way of disaster. Either Jack Morgan loves you like you are or he doesn't love you at all.'

'I guess he doesn't love me at all, then,' Bryony said bleakly. 'End of story.'

'But you're still going out there?'

'I want to see Maddy,' Bryony said, and she set her face. 'And Harry wants to see Jess. Maybe Jack Morgan won't be home.'

'Jessica needs to be mated.'

Ian McPherson, Myrna's husband, leaned on his tractor in the hot afternoon sun and looked at his friend in concern.

Yeah, right. Jessica needed mating. So Jack Morgan had driven ten miles over to Ian's place and then bumped his truck over the back paddocks to find him—just to tell him that? A telephone call would have worked as well. It couldn't be all Jack had to tell him.

There was no hurry. Let's go easy here, Ian told himself.

He stroked his dusty chin and stared out at the horizon, narrowing his eyes against the glare of the sun.

'I thought you and Jess were going for Australian champion?'

'Next year. Maddy and I have talked about it. Jessica's done enough shows for a while and Maddy thinks pups would be better than a trophy.'

Pups might stop Maddy asking for Bryony every second minute.

'Yeah, well, Ben's always willing to oblige a lady.' Ian clicked his fingers and a collie who looked very like Jessie came to heel. 'I assume that's what you want—to mate her with Ben?'

'Ben's the best dog in the district and almost as good a worker as Jess.' Jack leaned on the tractor beside his mate and stared at the horizon as well. He wasn't meeting Ian's eyes. 'We should end up with great pups. You want first choice of the litter as a stud fee?'

'I might. Myrna'll have a fit if I get another dog, but what the heck? It's time Fiona had a dog of her own to train.' Ian waved away a few flies. 'Jessica wouldn't have a bar of Ben last season, though. What makes you think she's changed?'

Jack shrugged. 'Nothing. But none of the other bitches have knocked Ben back. I'm hoping she'll be okay this time.'

'Some women are just plain fussy.' Ian bent to stroke his dog. 'Ben doesn't take offence easily, though, and he's always willing to try again.' He grinned. 'And again and again and again. I should have called him Casanova! When do you want him?'

'Jessie's just come into heat now. Maybe the day after tomorrow? I can pick him up if you like, and bring him back when he's through.'

'I'd appreciate it. I'm trying to get the fencing done before I get the hay in.'

'Yeah, right.'

Both men stared at the horizon. They'd known each other for ever, and there were things that needed to be discussed, but it was darn hard to start. Ian flicked a sideways look at his mate. Jack looked strained and tired, he thought. It'd been a real shock to Jack when he'd been landed with the kid out of the blue like that, but then, it had broken his heart when he'd lost her all those years ago.

So he had her back now. It wouldn't be Maddy that was causing the strain.

'Want to come up to the house for a beer? I've nearly finished here. What's left can wait until morning.'

'Nah.' Jack shook his head. 'I have to get back.'

He made no move to go. He stood still, staring at the distant hills as if they were really important. Ian chewed his lip. Somebody had to start things rolling.

'Seems Jessica's not the only one round here interested in mating,' Ian said quietly, and then stared at his boots for a while. And waited.

'Who told you that?' The strain in Jack's voice was obvious.

'Myrna.' Ian grinned. 'Who do you think? She tells me you and Bryony went to Melbourne together.'

That wasn't all Myrna had told him. She'd said Bryony had gone to Melbourne lit up like a birthday cake—and come back like a pricked balloon. All the joy had gone out of her.

'She's in love with him,' Myrna had told him, and because it was Myrna Ian believed her.

'Yeah,' Jack growled. 'We did.'

It wasn't an encouraging sort of statement. Still, the man had driven a long way to ask a simple question about mating a dog. The man must need to talk.

'She's quite a girl, our Bryony,' Ian said—and waited again.

'Yeah.'

This was like wringing blood out of stone. And then it came. Gushing!

'She is,' Jack said savagely. 'If you like scatter-brained, decorative pieces of fluff who flit from one man to another...'

'Hey,' Ian said, startled. 'Are we talking about the same girl here?'

'Bryony Lester.' Jack ground his teeth. 'There's only one Bryony. Thank God!'

'Well, I've known Bryony for almost as long as I've known Myrna.' Ian grinned. 'And yeah, I'll grant you she's scatter-brained. And decorative...' His grin deepened. 'Definitely decorative. But as for fluff...and flitting...'

'She's engaged to be married!'

Jack said the word 'married' in the same way he'd say she had the pox.

'Mmm.' Ian kicked the dirt. 'I heard that. Myrna says he's a suit.'

Jack let that pass. He didn't want to think about what the absent Roger was, suit or not.

'So what the hell is she doing kissing me, then?' he demanded. 'If she's engaged!'

'Did she kiss you?' Ian's voice was shocked but his eyes twinkled.

'Listen...'

'Did you kiss her?'

'Ian...'

'So what the hell were you doing kissing her when she's engaged to be married?' Ian asked mildly, and got it with both barrels.

'Because I wanted to. Hell, she's the most gorgeous...the most desirable... You just have to look at her to want—' Jack broke off and groaned.

'So you wanted to kiss her.' Ian nodded. 'And if she kissed you, then I assume she must have wanted to kiss you. You're two mature adults. I don't see the problem here.'

'I tell you, she's engaged!'

'But Myrna says she's been dating this Roger since she

was ten.' Ian pursed his lips thoughtfully. 'And she's not married yet. If I were you I'd go for it.'

'Ian…'

'You know, Myrna and I were hitched four weeks after we met,' Ian told him. 'We'd have done it faster if it was legal. But Bryony and Roger have been thinking about getting engaged for seventeen or eighteen years, and now they're thinking of getting married.'

'You're saying she doesn't want to marry him?'

'I'm saying if she's kissing other men there's definitely room for doubt.' Ian grinned. 'Hell, Jack, go for it. She's a ripper of a woman. I can't think of a woman I'd like to see you end up with more.'

'No!' Jack's denial was an explosion of violence.

'No?' A hundred or so flies were waved away in the great Aussie salute while Ian considered. 'Why not?' he asked at last.

Jack grimaced.

'Because she's just like Georgia.'

Ian thought that over, too. He bent and grabbed a piece of straw and chewed on it for a while. A sweep of white cockatoos rose screeching from a bank of gums down by the river, did a wide circle around the paddocks, and settled again.

'I don't see it,' Ian said at last. 'Georgia was five foot nothing, blonde and blue-eyed, looked like Dresden china.'

'Yeah, and Bryony's five-eight and red-headed, but they both don't belong here.'

'Bryony would if she married you.'

'Right. Like Georgia did.'

'Georgia was different,' Ian said carefully. 'Hell, mate, you must have realised by now that Georgia didn't want to marry you; she wanted to be on the stage. She wanted to be the centre of attention, and you were a bad second best.'

'Georgia was exotic and different from any other woman I'd known before,' Jack said harshly. 'Just like Bryony. Ian, I've sworn not to have anything to do with another woman.

I made that vow a long time ago. Well, now I have custody
of Maddy and Maddy needs a mother. I see that. But if I'm
marrying again, then I'll be marrying someone sensible.'

Ian's eyes narrowed.

'Like who?'

'Like Diana.' Jack's voice firmed. 'She belongs here. She
has all the skills I need...'

Diana...

'Yeah?'

Ian chewed his straw some more and thought about
Diana. He'd known Diana as long as Jack had. He'd even
dated her once. Once too often.

'I guess,' he said doubtfully. 'If we're talking skills, then
Diana learned to bob her hair and balance her sunglasses
on her forehead when she was twelve. Then she learned
dinner parties and she was as set for life as she wants to
be. I don't know if she knows a lot else. If that's the sort
of woman...'

'Hell!' Jack shoved off from where he was standing and
strode back to his truck, parked ten feet away. 'If you're
going to be offensive about the woman...'

'The woman you love?' Ian said quietly—and watched
his friend's face. 'Is that right, Jack?'

Jack looked as black as thunder. He didn't answer. He
climbed back into his truck, thumped shut the door and
jolted back over the paddocks as if he had invincible sus-
pension, with a firm resolve to get someplace fast.

'I just hope to hell he's not going to Diana's,' Ian muttered. 'I hope he has more sense than that.'

Jack wasn't home. Bryony arrived at Jack's farm on
Saturday afternoon to find Maddy alone with the housekeeper—a woman in her forties whom Bryony didn't take
to at all. The housekeeper was scrubbing the kitchen floor
when Bryony arrived. Maddy was clearly bored and lonely,
but she'd been told not to interrupt the importance of
kitchen-scrubbing.

'Daddy's gone over to see Mr Mcpherson and then someone else,' Maddy told her. 'I didn't want to go. Mrs Lewis
says I'm to keep out of her way and not bother her.'

'I see.' Bryony didn't see at all. Keep out of her way?
That was the last thing Maddy needed to be told. Bryony
felt like sacking Mrs Lewis on the spot.

'And I can't even play with Jessica,' Maddy went on,
looking at Harry as he raced around the garden searching
smells, looking for his love. 'She's in a cage out in the
shed by the haystack and Daddy says she's not to get out
or she might meet unsuitable dogs.'

'She's in season?'

'That's what Daddy says. He says she has to stay locked
up for a few days. He lets her out twice a day for a walk,
but he stays with her all the time when she's out.' Maddy's
face brightened. 'Daddy says she might have puppies in a
couple of months.'

'Might she?'

'Yes. He says I can have one, then I'll have two dogs
on my bed. Jessica and my puppy.' She gave a little skip,
immeasurably cheered by the prospect. 'It doesn't matter
about trophies if we have puppies. Puppies are better. Is
that all my stuff?' She eyed the little van Bryony was driving with delight. 'Can we take it to my bedroom now?'

'First things first.' Bryony rolled up her sleeves. If Jack
was away for the afternoon and Maddy was bored—well,
it was Saturday afternoon and Bryony was bored too, and
lonely. 'There's four cans of paint in the back of the truck,
and I brought paintbrushes and turpentine and overalls.'

She'd sort of hoped Jack might be here too, then they
could all have painted, but she and Maddy could have fun
together, despite Jack's absence. 'Want to help paint?'

'Oh, boy,' Maddy breathed. 'Yes, please.'

They completed a very satisfactory afternoon's work.

Mrs Lewis, pleased no doubt that Maddy was right out
of her way, graciously approved their activity, and at about

five o'clock—just as they finished the window ledges—she brought them up tea, lemonade and chocolate cake.

Maddy and Bryony fell on the food like the famished, and halfway through their second slice of cake Jack walked in.

He stopped at the door like a man struck.

'What on earth...?'

Maddy scrambled to her feet, delighted to see him. In her eagerness, she didn't see the dismay on his face.

Bryony did.

'Daddy, do you like my beautiful gold walls? We painted them ourselves. Bryony says she's got all the hangings for the bed and she didn't think you would have put the posts up yet, but she was really pleased you had because now she can put the hangings up and I can sleep in my Bryony bed tonight.'

'Tonight?' Jack's tone was astonished, and Bryony shook her head at Maddy.

'Only if it's okay with your daddy. It'll take about an hour to hang the silk and if Daddy's busy, then we'll do it another day.'

'The room smells of paint,' Jack said faintly. 'Surely Maddy can't sleep in here tonight anyway.'

'She can if the window stays open.' Bryony gathered her paintbrushes together and made her tone absolutely businesslike. 'But it's up to you if you want to wait. The walls need another coat, but you and Maddy can do that later. I've booked the carpet-layer for Thursday so that gives you four days.'

She rose to leave. And suddenly Jack couldn't bear that she go.

'You're very organising.'

'Bossy,' Bryony said, and met his eyes. 'Why don't you just say it?'

'Okay, bossy.' Jack gave a half-hearted grin. 'I'll agree with that. Miss Lester, do you know you have gold paint on your nose?'

That wasn't the only place Bryony had gold paint. Her jeans and old shirt were spattered everywhere. Maddy was worse. Mrs Lewis had found an old shirt of Jack's for the child, but Maddy's face was definitely golden.

'I have, too,' Maddy said proudly, pointing to a golden blob on the tip of her small nose. 'I got paint on my nose first because it was itchy and I forgot I had the paintbrush in my hand—and then Bryony said it looked very exotic and she put a blob on hers to match. And she said, "Now we're twins. The twit twins!"'

'The twit twins.' Jack's grin broadened. 'Well, Miss Lester certainly could have a point there.' He looked from Maddy to Bryony and back again. Two very gold noses gleamed at him, with laughter underneath, seductive in their warmth. He felt as if he was being hauled into a vortex of laughter. 'A spot of turpentine would get you two clean noses.'

'We like gold noses!' Bryony lifted a paintbrush. 'Are you jealous, then? Can we make it the twit triplets?'

'You just dare, Miss Lester.' He'd almost forgotten how threatening he found this lady. The vortex had hauled him right into the midst and he loved being there. Besides, how could he be threatened by one of the twit twins?

'Will you help us turn the bed into a canopy, then? Please, Mr Morgan?' Bryony smiled her most angelic smile—and took a threatening step towards him, gold paint dripping from her upraised brush.

Maddy giggled and raised her own brush.

'Yes! Yes. I give in.' Jack held up his hands in mock horror as Maddy burst into delighted chuckles.

'Just as well.' Bryony lowered her paintbrush and glowered, but she was starting to feel light inside again.

The lightness lasted for over an hour—until Diana arrived. Diana had obviously been invited for dinner. She arrived at six on the dot. When no one answered the door—Mrs Lewis had gone home as soon as Jack arrived—she let herself in and followed the sound of laughter up the stairs, and stopped at the door, staggered. The room had been transformed.

It was almost complete. The frieze and the wall hangings weren't up yet as the walls needed another coat of paint, and the carpet was yet to be replaced, but otherwise Maddy was perfectly and gloriously content. And the room was magnificent.

It shimmered and beckoned in gold and purple glory. The bed seemed to have grown. No longer an austere single bed, it was now a wonderful cavern that any little girl would give her back teeth for. Harry was settled contentedly in the midst of a sumptuous gold quilt, and a heap of stuffed toys spilled over the dog and onto the floor.

'Because a bed's not a bed without friends to share it with,' Bryony had declared. Having discovered Maddy was distinctly deprived in the stuffed-toy department—her mother hadn't packed any to send with her and Jack had provided one teddy and thought, manlike, that one was sufficient—Bryony had insisted Maddy choose a monkey and an elephant while they were in Melbourne. She'd then augmented the tribe with a few discards of her own.

'I've never thrown away a stuffed toy in my life and I keep buying them,' she'd explained, and, at Jack's look of incredulity, she'd sighed. 'Don't they look at you, Mr Morgan? Don't you just walk past a toy shop window and see them asking you to buy them?'

'I can't say I do...'

'Well, that's what happens to me,' Bryony had told him definitely. 'And I can't tell you what it's cost me to bring all my toys back from New York. I must have known there was a Maddy waiting here who needed them.'

She'd brought out an armload, hardly making a dent in her collection. So now there were pink gorillas with hats on, a vast woolly wombat, a battered lion—'Harry chewed the lion—he gave him a fright so he got his own back,' Bryony had explained—and various other bedtime friends.

The chandelier glimmered over their heads, but it wasn't lit now. There was a very special bedlight that Bryony had only just turned on. They'd hung the curtains—'They'll have to come down again when you do the second coat of paint, but what the heck? I want to see what they look like,' Bryony had also said—and had closed them to try out the light in darkness. The lamp rotated slowly, and from its shade a stream of moons and stars shone upwards onto the pale gold ceiling.

Gorgeous!

Diana didn't think so. She stood in the doorway and her eyebrows rose to the roof. She was dressed for dinner, simple but chic in black. Of course, black. The door jamb was still wet. Diana put her fingers on it, pulled them away in dismay, and looked down at them.

'The paint's wet,' she said, and Bryony managed an apologetic smile. She didn't like this woman—but maybe that wasn't all Diana's fault. Maybe it was because Bryony just knew Diana and Jack were such a suitable match.

Effort was required. She rose to her feet and handed her a rag soaked in turpentine.

'Hi, Diana. Do you like Maddy's bedroom?'

'No. I don't.' Diana ignored Bryony's outstretched rag with disdain and crossed to the bed. 'Jack, what on earth is this?'

Jack raised his brows.

'It's a bed, Diana,' he said mildly. Then he looked down at Maddy, who'd stopped mid-bounce with Harry on her lap. 'It's a very bouncy bed.'

'Have you taken leave of your senses?' Diana fingered the hangings and stared. 'Jack, this is silk!'

'Of course it's silk.' Jack's tone was faintly reproving, but Diana didn't hear the reproof. This woman had about as much intuitive sympathy as a mud-pat.

'You never paid good money for silk for a child's bedroom! Of all the ridiculous... Jack, she'll just spill things on it or rip it... What if her mother turns up again and demands she go back to the States? You'll have wasted all…'

Maddy turned white.

'I need to go to the bathroom,' she said—loudly. She grasped Harry around his middle, tugged him off the bed and carted him out of the room. Harry's head and backside sagged, but his tail wagged as they went. Maddy and Harry together, it seemed, were heading for the bathroom and, more, they were getting out of Diana's range.

Escape seemed like a very good idea to Bryony. Diana had every appearance of a woman here for the night, and Bryony had no intention of staying on as an unwelcome third.

'I need to go home, too,' she told Jack, ignoring the thunderous look he was giving Diana. He was welcome to blast Diana all he liked for her insensitivity—indeed, Bryony hoped he would—but not until Bryony was out of the way. 'I'll pack up and go but I'll leave you the paint. Bring me the brushes back when you're done—or I'll add them to my bill.'

'Bryony…' Jack cast a look at the retreating Maddy and Harry—and then he looked at Bryony. His look was almost a plea for help.

Sorry, mate, Bryony thought dully. She couldn't help him on this one. If Diana was the lady of his choice, then it was up to Jack to haul Diana into line.

'I'll see you later,' she said, and grabbed her stepladder.

'I'll help you to the car.'

Bryony shook her head.

'No. You've invited Diana for dinner, right? You need to cook. I need to go home.'

She had no reason to come back here now. No reason at all.

'The bill will be in the mail,' she said miserably as she took herself off out into the dusk.

*   *   *

She couldn't go home without Harry.

Bryony loaded her car and then went back into the house to find her dog. There was no Harry and no Maddy.

Jack was in the kitchen with Diana. He might have been annoyed a few minutes ago but he wasn't now. Bryony heard them laughing as she passed the kitchen door, and the sound made her feel bleak at heart. She had to fetch her dog and leave fast.

Maddy must still be in the bathroom. Sobbing her heart out, Bryony thought savagely, and swore at insensitive males who should have dumped their precious Diana and be outside the bathroom door, waiting.

'Maddy?'

She reached the top of the stairs and called. No one answered.

'Harry?'

Nothing.

She checked the bathroom and found it empty. Okay. They must have gone outside. She went out into the garden and called. The daylight was starting to fade.

'Harry!'

Still no Harry. Then Bryony saw Maddy stumping back towards her from the hayshed.

'Maddy?'

The child's shoulders were drooping and Bryony could see as she approached that Maddy had been crying. She waited until Maddy reached her. The child walked right up to her and then stood silent—waiting. Waiting to see if comfort was offered.

'She said my mother might come back and get me.' It was a sheer effort to get the words out and the pain behind them was dreadful. Bryony stooped and hugged her, then, because it seemed a good idea, she sat right down on the ground and hauled the little girl in closer.

'Well, that's a nonsense. If you think Jack will let you go, then you're a sandwich short of a picnic. Nuts! I hate to say it, Maddy, love, but I think Jack loves you much more than your mom does. And I think he has you now, and he's never going to let you go.' She smiled. 'Your daddy's just spent a fortune on your bedroom. Do you think he'd do that if he was going to let you go back to the States?'

Maddy considered, and some of the tension slumped out of her shoulders.

'He did spend a lot.'

'He certainly did.' Bryony blessed the silk shantung. If ever money had been well spent, Jack's had.

Maddy sighed. Things weren't completely okay yet.

'Diana said my bedroom was silly. She thinks I'm silly.'

'Well, that's okay. We *are* silly.'

'We...?'

'The twit twins. You and me. That's what we are. We should form a society of people who like squishy beds and gold noses and purple caves...'

Maddy gave a watery chuckle.

'You do like them, too?'

'Of course I do.' Bryony squeezed her hard. 'You know I do. If you're silly, then I'm silly, too. Sometimes silly is good, sometimes silly is even sensible. Your daddy's not going to let Diana change your room, so don't worry. Now, look up.'

'Look...?'

'So I can see your nose.'

Maddy looked, wondering.

'You have a very nice gold nose,' Bryony told her seriously. 'Do you know how Eskimos kiss?'

'H-how?'

'They rub noses. Gold to gold. Honest. A friend of Harry's told me that, and dogs know all about noses.' She leaned down and solemnly rubbed noses. Maddy giggled.

'That's better.'

But Bryony frowned inwardly, thinking of the future. She had to go home, and Maddy had to go inside, to face the dreaded Diana.

'Tell you what,' she suggested. 'If Diana's here often

you need to learn some cheering-up techniques, for times when Mrs Lewis or Diana tells you to be sensible.'

'Like what?'

'Well, squeezing Jessica or giving Daddy a cuddle is good.'

'Daddy's Diana's friend.'

'Yeah, but Daddy's silly inside, just like us,' Bryony promised her. 'You could almost make him an honorary twit. He just has to promise to be sensible around sensible people who do sensible things.'

'But he's with Diana now being sensible,' Maddy quavered. 'Jessie's locked up and I can't let her out, and you're going home.'

'Tell you what.' Bryony rose and took the child's hand in hers. 'I'll show you my favourite way I cheered myself up when I was six.'

'What did you do?'

'I climbed a tree.'

'Climbed...'

'It couldn't be just any tree,' Bryony told her. 'It had to be the biggest—the most splendid—the absolute king of climbing trees in the whole district. Are there any here like that?'

'I don't know...'

'What about that one?'

'That...' Maddy turned around to where Bryony was pointing—and gasped.

The tree was a vast river red gum. Its lower branches were close enough to the ground to get a leg up and keep climbing, but the branches rose so high you could get a stiff neck looking.

'I bet you could see for ever from that tree,' Bryony said thoughtfully. 'I bet you could see America. Or heaven. I bet you could almost talk to your grandma if you sat in that tree.'

'You think?'

'I definitely think. Come on. Let's climb.'

Bryony took off at a run towards the tree, and with a nervous little giggle Maddy followed.

Maddy forgot to be nervous as soon as she set her foot on the first branch. She climbed like a possum. Bryony was in front, but only just. They climbed and climbed. The tree was solid and comforting and the branches were spaced far enough apart to require concentration—but only just. There were handy forks to make resting places as they went, and the wide canopy of leaves was lovely in the still warm night under the setting sun.

Bryony called a halt about thirty feet above the ground.

'This is far enough,' she decreed, still looking up.

'It's awfully high.'

It was. There were some who'd say it was dangerous to let a child climb a tree this high, but Bryony had been raised in a farming community with no restrictions and no fear. Trees were made for climbing—the higher the better.

'Look out at the sunset,' she ordered. This had been the time she'd loved. With the fiery glow of the setting sun on the horizon, to sit in a tree and look out over your world was just about as close as Bryony could think of to heaven. She'd found peace there in the past.

Maddy, too. Bryony looked at Maddy's awed and wondrous face as she settled on the branch beside her and was satisfied. No matter how fussy Diana was in the future, no matter how troubled Maddy's world was, she had her bedroom and now she had this tree. Bryony knew that high in a gum tree was one place Diana couldn't reach her. You wouldn't see Diana in this tree. Some women were wimps.

'I guess it's time we went down,' Bryony told Maddy reluctantly. 'Harry will be wondering...'

She turned and looked down—and became a wimp all in the one movement. Mistake. Huge, fatal error! Bryony had last climbed a tree like this when she was fifteen years old, thirteen years ago. Thirteen years ago she'd been a fearless teenager. Thirteen years ago she hadn't known what high was. This was high. This was impossible.

She stared down through the branches to the ground below and all of a sudden things started to whirr. Spin. She closed her eyes—fast. Dear heaven...

'What's wrong?'

Maddy was watching her in concern.

'Nothing. Nothing, sweetheart.' It was hard to make her voice work.

Bryony opened her eyes again, and beads of sweat broke out on her forehead. She felt sick. She clung to her branch for dear life.

'Bryony, you look awful!'

She was scaring the child. She was scaring herself!

This is ridiculous, she told herself faintly. You've climbed trees like this since you were two years old.

They weren't this high. Yes, they were.

She was having a crazy conversation with a part of her she hadn't known existed.

It's an easy climb, Bryony. Just do it.

I can't climb with my eyes closed—and if I open them I'm going to fall.

She would, too. She knew that for sure. The feeling in her head—the dizziness—had to be psychological, but if she couldn't overcome it, it would make her fall all by itself.

Maddy was looking at her as if she couldn't understand at all. Maddy, sitting there without even holding on. Maddy, quite safe because she wasn't afraid.

Bryony's mouth was absolutely dry.

Just climb down without looking, she told herself, but she knew it wasn't going to work. She had to look down to find the next foothold. Oh, great. Just stay up the tree, then. For ever. Or call the fire department.

She gave a choke of hysterical laughter—then wrapped her arms very firmly around the branch she was sitting on and gripped for dear life.

'Maddy, I know this is really silly,' she managed. 'But

I'm feeling a bit funny, like my head is spinning. Do you feel like that?'

'No,' Maddy said blankly, swinging her legs back and forth over the abyss. 'I feel wonderful. I've never been this high up in all my life. I feel like a bird. Do you feel like a bird?'

'No.' Bryony wrapped her arms even tighter. 'I don't. Maddy, you don't know anyone with a fire engine, do you?'

'No.'

'I didn't think you would.'

There was nothing else for it. With an inward groan Bryony threw dignity to the wind, and she watched it fall. She held on tighter, with her toes as well.

'Maddy, you need to fetch your daddy,' she whispered. 'I think I need some help.' Fast.

CHAPTER NINE

IT TOOK Maddy a whole two minutes to swing her small
frame down to the ground, and Bryony couldn't believe
why her head wouldn't let her follow.

She was being absolutely ridiculous, but every time she
opened her eyes the same nauseous feeling flooded back
and threatened to overwhelm her. She couldn't even watch
as Maddy hit the ground and flew off to the house, pigtails
flying, yelling at the top of her lungs.

'Daddy, Bryony's stuck. Come quick. Help. Bryony says
she needs a fire engine...'

Oh, great! Mortification as well as terror. Diana was here,
too. Maddy's voice was so loud they'd hear her clean
across the river, but her urgency got results fast. Bryony
opened one eye a fraction of an inch and saw Jack burst
from the back door as if he'd been called to a bush fire,
Diana following. They looked worried.

Well, of course they were worried. Maddy was screaming for a fire engine. But they were all *down*. For Bryony,
looking down caused trouble all through her body. It made
her feel as if falling was inevitable. She closed her one eye
again.

'Is there a fire? Maddy, where's Bryony?' It was Jack's
voice from below, demanding, urgent—but suddenly im-
mensely comforting. If she couldn't have a fire engine, then
Jack would do. Minus Diana. Diana was an onlooker she
could do without!

'Good grief!' That was Jack's voice, raised in expletive
as he saw her.

Maddy must be pointing up the tree at Bryony. Heaven
knew what she looked like. She was lying full length on

her branch high in the tree, her arms and legs clinging like a sucker vine. She was clamped to that branch as if it were life itself, thirty feet up.

'Why on earth…?' Jack's voice was now just plain astounded.

'Bryony was teaching me to climb a tree,' Maddy explained, her voice tremulous. 'And she taught me really well because I went all the way up and it was beautiful. Bryony said I could talk to Grandma in that tree. But then she went all funny and started hugging the branch and asking about fire engines.'

The child's voice carried shrilly in the still, warm night.

Bryony was humiliated to her socks. There was nothing she could do about it. All she could do was wait, and cling. She heard them talk as they reached the base of her tree.

'For heaven's sake…' That was Diana. 'Why doesn't she just come down?'

Bryony hoped that, if she fell, she fell right on Diana.

'She can't.' Maddy's voice was scornful. Implied criticism of her wonderful Bryony was *not* allowed. 'She feels weird.'

'She is weird,' Diana said, and Maddy leaped to her friend's defence with a vengeance.

'She has to be weird. Silly. We're the twit twins. We're both twits. And Bryony says sometimes it's sensible to be silly. I'm going up again.' Maddy launched herself at the lower branches, only to be hauled back by Jack.

'No. You wait here, Maddy, love. Let me do this.' Then he called to the woman in the tree above him. 'Hold on, Bryony.' His voice held a touch of resignation—and humour—but also sympathy. 'I'm on my way.'

Jack reached her two minutes later and she didn't even see him come. By the time Jack touched her gently on the shoulder, Bryony was feeling sicker than she'd ever felt in her life before.

'Hey, Bryony.'

'Don't,' she whispered, her stomach churning and her

eyes tight closed. 'Don't tell me just to climb down. I know I should, but I can't. This is really stupid. I've climbed a million trees in my life.'

Tears of weakness trickled out from under her eyelids and she couldn't wipe them away, for she was holding on too hard to her branch. Jack did it for her. He leaned over and used his handkerchief to wipe her face, and then he was holding her shoulders, gently rubbing her neck.

'Hey, Bryony, there is no way you're going to fall.' His voice was infinitely gentle, infinitely reassuring. 'I'm here. I can hold you right onto the branch if I must, but there's no need even for that. This is a very safe tree. I've been climbing this tree since I was two years old. This branch is wide and strong and there's another wide, strong branch three feet under us.'

She knew that. She'd known that, anyway. Jack wasn't telling her anything new. But, illogically, some of the fear receded.

'Don't open your eyes,' Jack ordered. 'Not yet. I want you to sit up. I want you to let go your branch and let me hold you, and then I want you to look up at the sky. The evening star has just appeared. You can see it if you look up through the branches. Just let me hold you while you look.'

He pulled her back into his arms. It was the biggest test of courage—the biggest test of faith—that she'd ever had to face, to let go of that branch, to trust Jack.

But somehow... Somehow the pressure of his hands and the gentleness of his voice got through to the nerve-ends that were gripping her with terror. She released her vice-like grip and found herself enfolded against him. Her legs still gripped her branch but now she was sitting with Jack behind her, with her back curved in against his chest, and his broad arms held her tight.

One of his arms loosened, and pointed upwards. Before she could panic all over again he spoke, and his voice was roughly authoritative.

'See the star, Bryony. Look.'

She looked. The light from the star glimmered down through the branches and the soft golden hues from the sunset bathed them in a gentle light. And Jack's body was against hers.

'There's nothing to be afraid of. This is the most beautiful place on God's earth and I'm with you. You're not going to fall. No way. In a minute we'll go down together, but not until you've stopped shaking. So look at the stars and let me hold you and take long, deep breaths. Slow it all down.'

'J-Jack…'

'No. Concentrate on your star.'

Silence. Minutes passed and Jack didn't speak. The tremors that were racking her body eased away. She didn't want to move; she didn't want to move ever again. Here was where she wanted to be for the rest of her life.

But they had to go down.

'Okay, sweetheart, we're going down,' he said at last. Jack's mouth was against her ear. 'The only thing you are absolutely not to do is look down. Look up. Look out at the sunset or close your eyes. Or twist so all you can see is my shirt. But that's all you can look at. Right?'

'R-right.'

'Good girl. Look up—or out—or close your eyes or look at my shirt. Which?'

'Your shirt.' It was the best of a bad bunch by a country mile.

'Okay, twist.' In one deft movement he'd swung her round so she was cradled against him, her legs on the one side of the branch instead of straddling, hanging down.

'Okay. Put your hands on the branch. Don't look at it. Just feel it. I have your shoulders. Swing your left leg down until it touches the branch beneath. Right? I'm coming down too. Let your body stay against mine and your other foot will come too as we both lower ourselves. We'll end up on the next branch together and then we'll sit. Then we'll work onto the next branch. Piece of cake, Bryony. Let's do it.'

And somehow they did, with Jack talking her through every inch of the way and Bryony's face hardly leaving the solid barrier of Jack's broad chest. There was a button missing from his shirt and a splash of gold paint gleaming on the hairs of his muscled chest. By the time they reached the ground, Bryony knew that piece of gold so well she knew she'd see it in her dreams.

Then she was on the lowest branch, and Jack had swung down to the ground. He put his arms up and lifted her the final few feet. Her toes touched solid earth—and she sagged in a reaction of shame and overwhelming relief.

She would have fallen, but Jack still held her—tight. When she opened her eyes, all she saw was the gold on his chest again, but the ground was firm on her feet and the world had stopped spinning and God was back up there in his heaven. She was down here! Blow talking to Grandma ever again!

'Thank you...' she whispered in a voice that was still shaking, and then Jack was dropping a light kiss down onto her hair. It was a kiss of reassurance, nothing more, but it sure stirred Diana.

Diana had been watching with open-mouthed incredulity and now she gave forth like an angry dam-burst.

'Oh, for goodness' sake... This is supposed to be a famous interior designer! I don't believe it. A woman with no more sense than to get stuck up trees with children... Jack, if I were you I'd pay her what I owe her and get rid of her fast.'

'Yeah.' It was said absent-mindedly, as one brushed off flies. Jack's hands were still holding Bryony, and there was a shake behind his voice that matched hers. He put her away from him and held her at arm's length. 'Okay now, Bryony?'

'I... Yes. I'm fine. I'm so sorry. Diana's right. It was stupid.'

'It's not stupid,' he told her firmly. 'It happens. You think you're so in control of your head and then wham! The same thing happened to me once. I went caving. Four of us—one, two, three, four, like moles down a burrow. We went for what seemed miles, crawling on our bellies with a lantern apiece. A leader in front—Chris Roberts— then a mad caver called Angela Irvine, then me and Sam Carter last. I'd been down plenty of caves before and I was used to it.' He grimaced in remembrance.

'All of a sudden—and to this day I can't figure out how I got hundreds of yards before anything worried me—I suddenly thought, I've got someone behind me and someone in front and I can't get out. Can't even turn around. No way. I got cold sweats and found it hard to breathe. Angela was yelling from in front and Sam was shoving behind, but I froze and how they got me out I don't know. To this day I'm as embarrassed as hell about it—and it still brings back nightmares.'

Bryony stared.

She met the look in Jack's dark eyes and she knew he was telling the truth. He knew. He understood. With that one admission he'd let her off her humiliating hook, and Bryony was so grateful she could have kissed him. Or cried. But Maddy was hugging her legs—relieved but still unsure what all the fuss was about—and Diana was looking at her as if she were some sort of porriwiggle—and she had to move on.

'Well…thank you.' It was said formally but Bryony's eyes gave him their own message of thanks. She managed a quavering smile. 'I'll go now, before I cause any more trouble.'

Jack frowned. 'Are you okay to drive? You could stay and eat with us.'

And stay a porriwiggle? Bryony glanced at Diana—and glanced away.

'No, thanks.' She took a deep breath, gathering her tattered pride together as best she could. 'I'll just find Harry.'

Then she frowned as well. 'Hang on. I thought Harry was
with you, Maddy. He came out of the house with you?'

'Yes.'

Maddy tilted her chin, and found three adults looking at
her strangely. There was defiance in Maddy's tone. All of
them had heard it.

'Where is he, Maddy?' Jack asked, gripping his daughter's shoulder in an affectionate but firm grip. 'Have you
hidden him because you don't want him to go home? He
does need to go home, you know. He's Miss Lester's dog.'

'He stayed once before.'

'Yes. But tonight he's going home.'

Bryony could understand that! There was no way Jack
would want to deliver her dog home again. After tonight
there was no need to see each other ever again.

Maddy sighed. 'Really?'

'Really.'

Another sigh. 'Okay. He's in with Jess.'

'He's in…' Jack's voice was blank.

'With Jess,' the child repeated.

'You mean…in the shed with Jess.'

'In the cage with J—'

Maddy didn't finish the last word. Jack had turned and
was running across the yard with the urgency of a man with
a fire to attend. With a sinking heart, Bryony followed.

They were too late to stop anything happening.

Jack reached the shed first and flicked on the light.
Bryony came a close second with Maddy and Diana bringing up the rear. They all stopped at the shed entrance and
stared. Oh, no…

It was Maddy who broke the silence first. She pushed
her way through in front of her father, and her mouth
dropped open in fascination.

'Daddy, why is Jess stuck to Harry? Daddy, is there
something wrong?'

Nothing was wrong at all. Not for Jess, nor for Harry.

Bryony had never seen a pair of more self-satisfied dogs in her life. Any hope that the dogs might have only just joined was dashed immediately. Their passion was spent. As they watched, the dogs pulled reluctantly apart. Harry slumped away, exhausted, and Jess rolled over beside him on the straw, and started to lick her love.

A very satisfactory little interlude over, and if two dogs could be said to smirk Harry and Jessica smirked. Standing beside Bryony, Jack closed his eyes and didn't say a word.

'What's wrong?' Maddy demanded, anxious now. She knew from these three adult people that something major had happened here. She was an astute child.

'Maddy...' Jack's voice was weary. 'Didn't I tell you that Jess had to stay in the cage? That we had to keep her door locked?'

'Yes.' Maddy was still puzzled. 'But I did. I just let Harry in.'

'But I said...'

'You said she was in season and we had to keep her away from undes...' She faltered on the word. 'Undesirable dogs. Until we found a dog who could be a daddy for her pups. But Harry's not undesirable.'

Jack looked down at Harry's portly frame—at his bushy black eyebrows and his air of smug schnauzership—and he groaned.

'It'd be great if Harry was the daddy for Jessie's pups,' Maddy said definitely. 'Harry loves Jessica.'

'Madelaine!' Diana's voice was a douche of cold water over them all; even the dogs flinched. 'You know nothing about it. Jessica's worth thousands and thousands of dollars. If she's mated with a working dog with a good pedigree and the pups are trained before they're sold, they'll be worth thousands, too. And now... Now she's just mated with a mongrel!'

'Harry's not a mongrel. He's a schn...schn...'

'Schnauzer,' Bryony said bleakly. She slipped open the cage and retrieved her dog. Harry gave one exhausted wag of his tail and slumped in her arms—a thoroughly replete dog. 'I'm so sorry,' she told Jack, and she knew by the look on his face that things were just as serious as Diana had said. 'If there's pups...'

'There won't be pups,' Diana snapped. 'Jack will get rid of any resulting pregnancy. It'll mean he'll have to wait for the next season to mate her now, though.'

'What do you mean—get rid of any pregnancy?' Maddy demanded, her small hands on her hips and her eyes flashing fire. Then her eyes opened wide as her astute little brain worked things out. 'Do you mean...do you mean you want to kill Harry and Jessica's puppies?'

It was too much. Bryony closed her eyes and tried to think of something to say, and couldn't.

'I think I'd better go home,' she managed in a voice that was just above a whisper. 'I'm sorry.'

She looked at them all, but none of them was saying a word. Maddy was too shocked. Diana was smugly angry. Jack... Jack was just too stunned.

'Goodbye.' It was all she could think of to say. There was nothing else. She turned and walked back to her van—and no one tried to stop her.

What followed was a very bleak couple of weeks.

Bryony didn't see Jack or Maddy at all. Anything she knew about what was happening in their lives, she got from Myrna.

'Maddy's teacher says she's a much happier little girl now,' Myrna told her. 'Fiona tells me she carts a lion with a torn ear everywhere she goes, and she calls him Harry.'

At least she'd given Maddy that, Bryony thought miserably, and thought how much more she could give the little girl if she was allowed. She'd fallen hard in love with Jack Morgan—but she'd fallen pretty solidly for his little daughter, too. The thought of Diana as a mother for Maddy was truly horrible. No and no and no. Surely Jack had more sense?

'They seem an item,' Myrna told her sadly, knowing her friend needed to know the worst, no matter how bad it was. 'Ian says Jack's serious about getting married again.'

'Bully for Jack.'

'Oh, Bryony. You two seemed…well, so right…'

'Hah!' They were sitting on the front lawn of Myrna's farm, eating a pile of fish and chips Bryony had brought out from town. Hot chips were Harry's very favourite food. He had a system. One for Bryony, one for Harry. 'I can't even cook!' Bryony said, and her voice was bleak.

'There's more to marriage than cooking.'

'You can't live on fish and chips all your life.'

'I don't know,' Myrna said doubtfully. 'You and Harry seem to exist okay. Bryony, stop feeding that dog chips. He's getting as fat as a whale.'

'He loves me feeding him chips.'

'He'll love you just as much if you don't feed him junk food. And he'll live longer.' Myrna shook her head. 'Bryony, people are like dogs. They don't love you for things, or even skills. They love…they love you for *you*. If Jack loved you, then cooking wouldn't matter.'

'Try telling Jack that. He's all fired up for a sensible bride.' Bryony rolled over on the grass and ate six chips in quick succession. 'Anyway, who's to say he loves me? He doesn't even like me. I'm a flibbertigibbet.'

'But you love him.' Myrna reached over and took her friend's hand in hers. 'And don't think I haven't noticed you're missing an engagement ring. Even Fiona knows. I was putting her to bed last night and she said, ''How come Aunty Bryony's not wearing her engagement ring any more?'' You can't wear a rock for months and then expect people to ignore its disappearance.'

'You haven't noticed up till now.'

'Yes, I have,' Myrna said gently. 'I just figured you'd tell me in your own sweet time.'

'Like now?'

Myrna grinned and poured Bryony a glass of wine. Ian

was away at an agricultural field weekend so informality was the order of the day.

'Yeah. Like now.'

Bryony sighed. 'What is there to tell? We're not engaged any more.'

'Because of Jack?'

Bryony sighed again. 'Because of Jack.'

'But you and Jack...'

'I know.' Bryony stared gloomily into the bottom of her wine glass. 'There's no future in me and Jack. But you're right when you say I love him. No matter how he feels. I lust after the man. I can't look at him without my knees turning to jelly. If he asked me to marry him tomorrow— heck, Myrna, if he asked me to go to bed with him tomor- row—there's no way I'd knock the man back. He feels... He feels...'

'I know,' Myrna said gently. 'You don't have to tell me. I feel the same way about Ian.'

Bryony gave her a shamefaced grin. 'Embarrassing, isn't it?'

'No.'

Of course it wasn't. Not for Myrna, because Ian felt the same way back. But for Bryony...

'Well, I couldn't stay engaged to Roger feeling like this,' she said. 'It wasn't fair, and Roger didn't really mind. I was like a nice comfortable habit he's had for years, and now he's going to think seriously about the bride of his choice. I might just have done Roger a favour by not mar- rying him.'

'I see.' Myrna stood up to peep in the pushchair at the sleeping twins. The two older children were playing on a trampoline under the trees. She turned to look at them, to not look at Bryony. 'So where does that leave you now? You were going to stay here until I stopped breast-feeding the twins and then marry Roger. Will you go back to New York now?'

'I don't know.'

'You're welcome to stay here as my partner for as long as you want,' Myrna suggested.

'No.' Bryony shook her brilliant curls. 'Apart from the agency not being big enough to support you and me full-time…'

'It is!'

'It is not. Two part-timers or one full-time…but I need more than part-time work, and to be honest…'

'To be honest, you prefer to leave,' Myrna said quietly. 'Do you want to leave straight away? It must almost be killing you to watch Jack and Diana…'

'No.' Another head-shake. 'You're still breast-feeding and there's no way you can operate the agency without me.'

'It doesn't matter…'

'It does.' Bryony set her face. 'I promised you another few months and you'll have that. It'll give me time to sort out what I want to do—maybe set up an agency in Melbourne. I need to think about it.'

'Oh, Bryony…'

'Don't you dare feel sorry for me.' Bryony ate another chip, biting it off at finger level as if a spot of viciousness would do her good. 'Don't!'

'Well, what are you going to do for the next six months? Besides interior design, that is. You can't just lie around and eat chips and pine.'

Harry ate the tail-end of Bryony's chip, and wagged his ample rump. Bryony looked at him and considered. She really did need something else to think about, or she'd go quietly nuts.

'I know,' she said at last. 'We'll have a mission. Harry and I will cease eating chips. Harry will diet, and we'll do an obedience course. Me and Harry. Then we're going back to one of those damned dog shows and we're going to win a ribbon. If that's not something great to aim for, then I don't know what is.'

Harry looked adoringly up at his mistress—and ate another chip.

'Jack goes to the dog shows,' Myrna told her.

'So what?' Bryony tilted her chin. 'We just might even beat him at his own game.'

Fat chance!

CHAPTER TEN

BRYONY'S resolve to ignore Jack Morgan and get on with her own life lasted a whole three days.

Three days later, as she sat on the rugs in her front room drawing up a colour scheme for a client, Jack Morgan knocked on her front door and Bryony's resolve to be independent and blasé and a woman for whom men were a thing of the past turned to tatters again. She just had to look at Jack Morgan to wilt at the seams. Men in general might be a thing of the past. This was no man in general. This was Jack!

It didn't even matter that he was angry, and he *was* angry, she could tell that the moment she looked at him. When she opened the door, Jack stalked into the living room and actually ignored Harry's exuberant greeting. The toad! Dear heaven, she loved him.

'Jessie's pregnant.'

As an opener it was a definite attention-grabber.

'Oh. I see.' Bryony swallowed. 'It's Harry, then.'

'Of course it's Harry. I didn't even bother to mate her with any other dog. You've cost me thousands.'

That wasn't completely fair. Bryony looked at it from all angles and decided not to hang her head completely.

'It was your daughter who put them together,' Bryony reminded him gently. 'But if you'd like to sue...'

She'd thought about this over the past few days. If Jack was short of money then maybe she'd consider some sort of compensation, but Myrna had assured her that Jack Morgan was so rich, the money he earned from his breeding programme was peanuts.

'You're saying it was Maddy's fault?' Jack was stirring

himself up, fuelling his rage. His face was as black as thunder.

'Yes.'

'How dare you…?'

'Oh, come on!' Bryony flopped onto one of her sofas and eyed her love with a trace of humour. 'You'll never win a court case on this and you know it. Kids and dogs get up to mischief. They always have. They always will. Your kid let my dog into your dog's cage, and Harry had his wicked way. The way Harry and Jess get on, we should have seen it coming. We didn't, but what's happened can't be mended by anger, so stop ripping at me and tell me what you're planning to do. Get the pups aborted?'

'No.'

The thunder remained. Jack stared down at Bryony, baffled. She was a gypsy this morning, her red skirt flouncing down to her ankles and her tight little knit top, with scoop neck and no sleeves, showing off her figure to perfection. She had about five gold bracelets on her wrists again and a couple more on her ankles, and there were wide gold hoops hanging from each ear under her curls.

A man could go mad with wanting, she was so lovely! But *totally* impractical. Jack's mouth set in a tighter line. He knew what he had to say and he was going to say it, then he was going to leave.

'If it wasn't for Maddy, I'd get rid of the pups,' he said heavily. 'But the child's emotionally involved.'

The child…

Bryony's face stilled. That sounded like Diana.

'She can keep one of the pups for a pet. The others… Well, we may be able to sell them as pets if they don't look too ridiculous, but half of them can be your responsibility.'

The child…

The word had cut Bryony to the bone.

'Fine.' Bryony hoisted Harry into her arms and stood up, and glared. 'Harry and I take our responsibilities very seriously. He's the father, so of course we'll raise our share of the pups—in fact, we'll raise all of them if you want—and we won't call any single one of them "the child" once.'

'What do you mean by that?'

'Meaning you sound like a toad when you call Maddy "the child",' she snapped. 'You sound like Diana. Or Mrs Lewis. As cold as a wet fish. For heaven's sake, Jack Morgan, don't let them rub their coldness off onto you, or Maddy's going to be miserable.'

'I don't know what you mean.'

'Yes, you do,' she flung at him. 'Oh, they're efficient, both of them. They'll run your house and your life in ordered harmony; you won't be bothered by a thing. You won't catch them making mud pies in the bath...'

'Mud pies in the bath...?' Jack paused, astounded.

'I had the flu once and couldn't go outside for days so my mom let me make mud pies in the bath,' she told him obscurely. 'And my dad came in to help. It was the best day! I'll remember it for ever. Would your Diana help Maddy make mud pies in the bath?'

Jack stared.

'No. Of course she wouldn't,' Bryony went on inexorably. 'And Mrs Lewis wouldn't let you carry a bucket of mud over her kitchen floor.'

'And you would?'

'Of course I would.' Bryony hoisted Harry higher and they glared together. Harry set his hairy eyebrows close and tried for a statesman-like approach. It didn't quite come off. Dignity wasn't his strong point. Combined, though, they were quite a force.

Jack took a step back.

'I hear you've broken off your engagement,' he said flatly, changing tack. 'Fiona told Maddy at school.'

'So?' Despite her fast rejoinder, Bryony was starting to feel like a squashed puffer fish. She felt ill.

'Have you?' His voice was a cold demand for the facts.

'I have.' There was nothing else to say. Jack was cold and angry and...and not really the least bit interested.

His face hardened even further. 'You needn't think it'll make any difference!'

Now *that* was the outside of enough. Her puff swelled back. Temper was a definite help here.

'Of all the arrogant, autocratic, conceited... What makes you think my engagement has anything to do with you, Jack Morgan?'

'It hasn't anything to do with me,' he agreed flatly.

'Well, then. Butt out!'

He glared to match hers. 'Okay, I will. But you're a fool if you don't marry your Roger.'

'What on earth would you know about Roger?' Bryony demanded. Boy, was her temper helpful!

'Only what you've told me, and what Myrna and Ian have told me. That he's a sensible, hardworking man who's been loyal to you for years. He doesn't deserve to have his ring flung back in his face.'

'I didn't fling...'

'Bryony...' Jack's voice cracked. He took a hasty step towards her and grabbed her arm.

Bryony looked down, and a tiny hope swelled in her heart. But the hope didn't last long. It had about two whole seconds to live.

'Bryony, that interlude in the hotel...'

Bryony took a deep breath. 'You mean—the interlude when you kissed me?'

'Yes.'

Interlude. Her eyes flashed. 'What of it?'

'It was a mistake,' Jack said heavily. 'It doesn't mean anything. Now or then.'

'So why are we talking about it?'

'Because if you've split up with Roger because of it...'

'I haven't split up with Roger because you kissed me. Not just that.' Bryony steadied. She had a choice here. She could shut up, or she could say what was in her heart, and Bryony had always followed her heart.

'I split up because I've fallen in love with another man,' she said, her voice gentling as her anger faded. 'I've fallen in love with you, Jack Morgan, and marrying Roger wouldn't be very fair when I'm in love with another man—now would it?'

'Bryony...'

'Yes?' Her voice was almost a whisper. Jack's was hoarse and full of pain. He let go of her wrist and Bryony stared down at the marks his fingers had made. They'd fade, she told herself, and she was about to be left with nothing.

'I don't love you,' he said.

His voice was flat. Despairing. Defenceless.

'I think you're a liar, Jack Morgan,' Bryony said gently—and she placed Harry on the floor and reached out to touch his face with the palm of her hand. 'I think we knew the moment we met that there was something between us.'

'Yes. There was.' He thrust her away with a sound that was half moan, half growl. 'Hell, Bryony, I want you—but I don't want you as my wife.'

'So what do you want me as, then?' she demanded. 'You won't take me to bed. You don't want to kiss me. You don't want to marry me. What do you want?'

'I just want...' Jack shook his head, bewildered. 'Look, this doesn't make sense. I'm in this way over my head and I have to get out.'

'Get out and back to Diana?'

'*Yes!*' It was practically a shout and, startled, Harry gave a threatening woof at their feet. 'Yes. Diana's sensible.'

'Diana's boring.'

'She won't walk out on me.'

Bryony closed her eyes, and when she opened them she knew what she had to do. She walked over and opened the door.

'Believe it or not, Jack Morgan, neither would I,' she said, and her voice was none too steady.

'That's what you say now. That's what Georgia said.'

'So you'll believe Diana—but you won't believe me.' She shrugged. 'Jack, this is hopeless. If you don't trust, then you don't love and there's nothing more to be said. End of story. Believe it or not, I've exposed myself more to you than I've exposed myself to anyone in my life before. But that exposure's finished now. I know when I'm beaten. Please leave, Jack Morgan. You're no longer welcome in my house. You're no longer welcome in my life.'

She stood and waited—until Jack Morgan walked out of the door. Walked out of her life for ever.

In the next few weeks Harry lost two kilograms and learned to walk on a lead without wrenching Bryony's arm off. He learned to heel, to sit, to drop, to fetch and altogether behave in every way like a totally civilised dog. In fact, he appeared to enjoy it.

'He's a real pleasure to help train,' the local obedience-school manager told Bryony, and it was the only bright spot of a bleak month.

'You're keeping me sane,' she told her newly docile pet one evening as she took him for his third walk of the day, but she knew it was no such thing. Harry wasn't keeping her sane. He was keeping her busy, but sanity was a long way off. She'd heard absolutely nothing from Jack.

'At least there's been no engagement notice,' Myrna told her the next day, troubled. 'And Maddy seems happy enough at school.'

'Mmm.'

'Bryony, do you want to leave here sooner than you intended?'

'I'll stay for four more months,' Bryony told her. 'I promised I'd be here until the twins stopped breast-feeding and I'll honour my promise. And besides,' she added bleakly, 'I can't think where else to go.'

That was the closest she'd come to cracking in front of anyone, to admitting how heavily she'd fallen for a pair of laughing eyes and gentle, farmer hands. Myrna hugged her friend, then put the kettle on and watched her with anxious eyes as they drank their coffee. Harry wasn't the only one losing weight.

'You're not going into a decline, are you, love?'

Bryony considered the possibility. 'A decline... I hadn't thought of that.' She grew more cheerful at the thought. 'My only white outfit hasn't been the same since I got cow dung on it. Can I look wan and palely loitering without it?'

'Wafting around waif-like in search of a boat full of flowers and a lake wherein to end it?' Myrna chortled. 'I hardly think so. No, I guess you haven't quite come to that.'

'I might. I quite fancy myself dying of a broken heart.'

'Then who gets to feed Harry?'

'There is that,' Bryony conceded. She picked up her dog and grinned. 'Okay. I won't decline. Floating till my boat sinks wouldn't work for me anyway. I just know I'd tread water for days rather than slipping to the lake's muddy bottom like a wimp. And the alternatives—well, guns are so noisy they give me a headache, and rope necklaces are definitely not a fashion statement. The only way I'll die is from hunger. Harry and I haven't eaten a chip for weeks.'

'And it's doing you both good,' Myrna said roundly. She smiled, but inwardly she had her doubts. 'How's the dog training going?'

'Just wonderful. Come on, Harry. Show Aunty Myrna your stuff.'

And Bryony put Harry though his paces. Harry performed like a circus trouper, and beamed at the end of it.

'Goodness.' Myrna was absolutely astounded. 'I never knew he had it in him. I must admit I thought all he was good for was eating and sex!'

'Well, we're both off food and sex,' Bryony said definitely. 'So there has to be something else out there for abstainers like us.'

Myrna was no longer listening. She was thinking, out loud.

'Bryony, there's another dog show next Saturday week up at Horsham. Why don't you try showing Harry again?'

'You have to be joking! Look at the trouble it got me into last time.'

'That was with an untrained dog. But now... Bryony, Harry's pedigree's impeccable and he's lost weight and he behaves himself. If he wins... Well, it'll help you sell these pups Jack's landing on you.'

'Oh, yeah. Champion mother and father, just not the same breed.'

'It'll still help,' Myrna said stubbornly. 'Fiona wants one but Ian won't let her have it if he doesn't think Harry's a decent dog. You have to prove he's trainable or we'll have to look elsewhere for Fiona's pet.'

Bryony glared. 'Myrna, that's blackmail.'

'That's right.' Myrna gave Bryony her very sweetest smile. 'Blackmail's what I'm principally best at, just ask Ian. Come on, Bryony, you've been wearing a groove round and round the block over the past few weeks, walking your darned dog. This will get you out of the house, get you meeting more people.' She brightened. 'Who knows? There might be a stud dog with a stud owner to match in the ring right beside you.'

'Yeah?'

'Yeah.'

That was something to think about, but it would have to be some stud to match Jack Morgan.

Bryony filled out three separate entries to the show and ripped them up before she finally worked up the courage to send one. At the back of her mind was her biggest niggle. What if Jack was there? He wouldn't be there with Jessica, she knew. Jess must be near term. But he might be showing another dog.

It didn't matter. The sheepdogs did their stuff on the other side of the showground from the pedigree trials.

She and Harry could pick up their blue ribbon and leave. Fast. Anything was better than sitting here watching the walls close in, going quietly crazy!

They didn't win a blue ribbon, but they won red. Red for second prize. Bryony had gone conservative, in neat grey trousers and white blouse so as not to intimidate the judges—'They don't like different,' Myrna had told her—and Harry had been groomed till he gleamed—but in the end a smart little female schnauzer with a smug expression and an owner with a blue rinse and a Mercedes carried off the honours.

It didn't matter. Second was great. Bryony was so proud of Harry, she was close to bursting. Myrna was in the crowd with Ian and the children and they all clapped until their hands ached—and Bryony wondered how solidly Myrna had sent home the message. Cheer Bryony!

It didn't matter. She was cheered. She draped the red ribbon proudly around Harry's neck and they walked from the ring six inches taller than when they'd entered.

'Bryony! Bryony! Harry came second. He was terrific!'

It was a frantic yell from the side of the ring and Bryony stopped dead. She knew that voice. Maddy. Then Maddy was beside her, kneeling in the dust to hug Harry and let him lick her all over. She looked bouncy and healthy and very cute in the same red trousers she and Bryony had chosen together. 'Oh, you clever dog,' she told Harry, hugging him close. 'I knew you were smart. I've missed you.'

She looked accusingly up at Bryony. Bryony wasn't coming at that. She couldn't use a guilt trip as well as everything else. She looked accusingly right back.

'You shouldn't be here on your own. Where's your daddy, Maddy Morgan?'

'Here.'

Bryony jumped a foot, and when she came down to earth

Jack Morgan was standing right behind Maddy—with Diana in tow.

'Oh.' Bryony struggled a bit for air. 'Hi.'

Jack didn't answer. He left the reply to the lady at his side.

'Hello, Bryony.' That was Diana at her condescending best. Squattocracy mingling with the peasant classes, sweeping her hair from her face and adjusting her sunglasses. 'Did you see my mother's dog just now?' she asked pleasantly. 'She's the one that won.'

Of course.

'But Harry did really well,' Maddy said proudly.

'Yes, dear, he did.' Diana took Maddy's hand and made her stand up. Firmly. Patronising cow! 'Come on, Madelaine. You know we want to see the craft.'

Maddy cast an appealing glance up at Bryony, and then she looked behind Bryony to where Myrna and her brood were descending on them *en masse*.

'Can I stay with you for a while?' she pleaded urgently to Bryony. 'I don't want to go to the craft with Diana.'

Diana opened her mouth to say no, but Myrna's Fiona saw her friend Maddy and whooped with delight. Then Ian arrived to talk to Jack, and somehow it was decided that Jack and Ian would go and inspect the bulls and Diana and Myrna would take the twins and check out the craft and Bryony would take the older children—Fiona and Maddy and Peter—on the Ferris wheel.

Bryony said nothing while the organisation went on around her. Okay. It was okay. The world wouldn't open up and envelop her just because Jack Morgan was looking at her, she just wished it would.

Bryony escaped finally, with three kids and a dog in tow. She felt as if she'd been through the wringer and Jack hadn't said a word to her.

Never mind. Bryony and three kids could have fun even if she was miserable, she decided crossly. Even if Jack had brought Deadly Diana to the show.

So Bryony threw herself heart and soul into having fun.
And they did. They ate candy floss. Bulk candy floss. The
kids fed ping-pong balls into clowns' mouths and won
junk—and then they held Harry while Bryony fed ping-
pong balls into clowns' mouths and didn't win anything at
all. They ate a toffee apple apiece and then checked out the
Ferris wheel. The kids thought it looked tame.

For Bryony it looked just the opposite. Bryony thought
it looked high—and she was newly respectful of heights.

'What we really want to go on, Aunty Bryony,' Fiona
confided, noting her reluctance with approval, 'is the
Tunnel of Doom.'

'The Tunnel of Doom...'

Bryony hardly got the words out of her mouth before six
eager hands were hauling her across the showground. They
knew a soft touch when they saw one.

Bryony knew a mistake when she saw one. She checked
out the Tunnel of Doom in horror. It looked innocent
enough on its little parking lot. A cute little train with ten
carriages. Only the wire cages over the top of each open
carriage and the triple-anchored seat belts inside said it
mightn't be quite as innocent as it looked.

Then Bryony checked out the tunnel. It was like a vast
caterpillar rolling up into the air in vast hoops—twisting
right over in hundred-and-eighty-degree turns. She would
have killed to go in this when she was six years old. Yeah,
well, she'd climbed trees when she was six years old; now
she felt about a hundred.

'Can we go on it, Aunty Bryony? Can we, please...?'
Fiona and Peter were actively pleading. Maddy had that
unmistakable look about her again. Yearning. Even Harry
looked excited.

'If you think I'm getting on that... And you can't go by
yourselves... And Harry isn't allowed...'

'Yes, he is, miss,' the attendant said helpfully. 'Dogs
love it. We can strap them in with you or on their own.
Look at my Boof!' He pointed to a large black Labrador

strapped into one of the carriages. 'Rides around in it all day, he does, and he never tires of it. Come on—give it a whirl.'

Whirl? Dear heaven...

Then, somehow, she found herself paying her money and being towed mercilessly forward. Two carriages. Peter and Fiona in front, beaming, Maddy and Harry and Bryony in the rear, Maddy and Harry beaming. Bryony staring fixedly ahead. She felt even older than a hundred. Then they all took off and everyone stopped beaming. They screamed instead.

Even Harry screamed. Bryony was sure she heard him, though how she could hear anything above the sound she was making herself was a very interesting point, if anyone was interested, and Bryony wasn't. All she was interested in was holding onto her stomach until the damned thing stopped.

Finally it did. The train rolled to a halt, the kids all jumped out, and they started beaming all over again.

'That was fantastic. *Fantastic! Ace! Cool!* Can we go again, Aunty Bryony? Please?'

'N-no.' Bryony staggered over to a seat, a mercifully stable seat, on solid ground, with no horrid little wheels or cages, or tunnels. 'I've run out of money. Thank you, God, for not letting me bring more.'

Her legs sagged from under her—and so did Harry's. He lay in her lap and even his moustache dropped. With one eye he glared out at the Labrador still sitting benignly in his carriage as they loaded the next lot of passengers—as though it were some sort of a dummy dog put there to dupe innocent schnauzers.

'There you are!' It was Myrna's voice and Bryony managed to raise her head high enough to see Myrna, Ian, Diana and Jack all bearing down on them, the twins' pushchair in front. 'We've been looking all over for you.'

'We've been in the Tunnel of Doom,' the kids yelled in unison, and out of what was left of her consciousness

Bryony was aware that Maddy was jumping up and down in excitement too. It really was extraordinary—the change that had come over this little girl in the last two months. Maddy knew Jack loved her. A change would come over Bryony, too, if she knew Jack loved *her*.

Heavens, for something like that—for Jack's love—she'd even get into the Tunnel of Doom again!

Now Maddy was tugging her father's hand with urgency. 'Bryony's run out of money and we really want to go in there again. Please, Daddy.'

Jack looked at Bryony—and grinned. 'Does Bryony want to go again?'

'It's your turn and I wouldn't deprive you for the world,' Bryony managed, turning green. 'Harry and I have had enough treats for one day.'

'We all have,' Diana said firmly. 'I don't think rides like this are good for children. They upset their stomachs.'

'Don't talk about stomachs,' Bryony pleaded.

'Harry wants to go again.' Maddy grabbed Harry around his middle, hauled him into her arms and swung him around to face her father. 'Don't you, Harry?'

Harry didn't. He coughed, and Maddy looked doubtfully down at him.

'Put that dog down!' Diana ordered.

Maddy turned to her.

'Why? Don't you like Harry? He's a nice dog. See his eyebrows? He's got the best eyebrows of any dog I know.' And she held him out for Diana to inspect them.

Harry coughed again—with results. Someone must have fed him candy floss. Oh, dear... Diana's trousers were cream. Or, rather, Diana's trousers had been cream. Now they were pink, with little bits of green in between.

Diana's scream was louder than Bryony's on the Tunnel of Doom. She screamed long and hard, and then there was silence. The silence went on and on into infinity.

Bryony bit her lip, bit her tongue—bit everything to try

and stop hysteria rising. Dear heaven, she couldn't laugh.
She mustn't. But...for this to happen...to Diana...

Thank you, God, Bryony said silently for the second time
in two minutes. She held her hand to her mouth and sank
back down on her seat—and closed her eyes. It couldn't
have happened to a nicer person.

Oh, help... She was going to laugh. She must! Just pretend you're unwell yourself, Bryony, she decided desperately, because if you laugh you're never going to get out
of this alive.

'Oh, no...' Myrna was the first to speak. Her voice was
decidedly unsteady and Bryony thought it was wisest to
cover her eyes with her hands as well as her mouth. If she
looked at Myrna...

'Ugh! That's *dis...gusting!*' That was five-year-old
Peter. 'I told you not to feed him candy floss, Fiona. Now
he's puked all over Diana.'

'Don't say puke...' That was Ian. His voice shook, too.

'I think... I think we need to go home.' Jack's voice was
even more uneven than Ian's, and Diana swivelled to glare
at him.

'No!' It was a chorus from all the children.

'It's okay, we can wash it off here,' Maddy said helpfully. 'When Bryony got cow dung on her, we got one of
the farmers to squirt her with the hose.'

'Jack...' It was a dire warning. Diana's voice was laced
with pure venom.

'Jack, you'd best take Diana home,' Myrna managed,
trying to deflect Diana's mounting fury as well as keep a
straight face herself. There was no way Bryony could say
anything and Ian wasn't much better. 'We'll bring Maddy
home with us later.'

'I'd appreciate that.' Jack's laughter was dying. Diana's
venom was a real laughter-quencher.

'Please do.' Diana stared down at her ruined trousers and
then directed her venom straight at Bryony. 'That would be
fine. Just get me away from this woman. Fast. Wherever

she goes, there's trouble. The sooner she moves away from this town, the better it'll be for everyone concerned.'

Bryony was starting to think that, too. She sat at home that night and nursed a recuperating Harry. Actually, Harry was fine. Once rid of the candy floss he'd cheered up immediately and even tried to follow Diana. Well, she was now carrying *his* candy floss... The dog was a definite liability.

'Just lucky I love you,' Bryony said miserably, and tucked herself into her big and lonely bed with a glass of muscat and a large bar of chocolate, and Harry. 'Blow the diet tonight. We both need cheering up.'

Just before midnight—when they both should have been asleep but Bryony was staring at the ceiling thinking miserable thoughts of what she intended to do with the rest of her life—the phone rang. Bryony's heart went straight to disaster. Interior designers' phones didn't ring at midnight.

It had to be her parents. Something had to be wrong. She was so distressed already that it took a whole two seconds—the time to turn the light on and lift the receiver—for Bryony to convince herself that both her parents were road kill.

It wasn't her parents. It was trouble for Maddy!

The voice on the end of the line was Diana's.

'I just thought you should know the damage you've caused,' she said, and the venom of the afternoon was still there.

'Damage?' Bryony stared blankly at the phone. 'Oh, you mean the pants. Diana, I *am* sorry. I'll pay for them.'

'I don't mean the pants, you stupid woman,' Diana snapped, and there was a nasty little thread of smugness behind the words. 'I mean Maddy. I told you that ride would make the children ill.'

Bryony sat bolt upright.

'Ill? Maddy's ill?'

'She couldn't eat tea,' Diana told her with satisfaction. 'Then she vomited; not just once, either. She kept right on vomiting. Jack and I had to bring her into hospital and it's all down to you, Miss Lester. So I hope you're feeling really pleased with yourself.'

She slammed down the phone, and Bryony was left staring at the wall. She stared at it for a whole three seconds. Then she leaped to her feet, dragged on a tracksuit and headed for the hospital.

CHAPTER ELEVEN

THEY wouldn't let her in.

Bryony hit Casualty with the force of a small bulldozer, but she was baulked at Reception by a nurse who wasn't impressed by small bulldozers. Army tanks wouldn't work against this implacable front.

'I'm sorry.' The nurse was pleasant and kindly—but as immovable as solid steel plate. 'Maddy's undergoing procedures in one of the minor theatres at the moment.' She nodded at a pair of swinging beige doors behind her. 'Through there. I'm afraid you can't see her.'

'But what's wrong?'

'I'm afraid I don't know. They're still running tests.'

'Is she seriously ill?' Bryony managed, and at the look on the nurse's face she didn't need an answer.

Dear God.

'Can you tell me what's happening?' she whispered. 'Please…'

The nurse shook her head. 'I can't. I really know very little more than I'm telling you. Look, if you'd like you can sit in the waiting room, and I'll ask Mr Morgan if he'll see you when he can leave his daughter for a moment.'

'Yes, please,' Bryony said numbly—and sat. And sat. For hours. There was nothing happening in Casualty. It was Saturday night but the boys on the town must have been behaving themselves. The silence just got more and more ominous. The Dragon Lady did paperwork behind her desk and watched Bryony out of the corner of her eye.

The phone rang. Dragon Lady answered and Bryony strained to hear.

'Diana… Hello, how are you? No, there's no news yet.

159

I'll ring you when we know something, shall I? No? Oh, I see. Yes, I expect you will be more help if you get some sleep. In the morning, then? Sleep well.'

Fat lot you care, Diana Collins, Bryony thought bitterly. You should be here, you cow! If you're going to be Maddy's mother... The thought was unbearable.

What might be happening on the other side of those beige doors was starting to be unbearable. This wasn't sounding like a normal tummy bug. Bryony was getting more and more frightened by the minute.

She put her head in her hands and closed her eyes—and when she opened them the nurse was standing above her with a cup of tea.

'You could use this, I think,' she said, and something about her had changed. Something had softened.

'Thank you,' Bryony said, and managed a smile.

'I've heard about you,' the dragon lady told her. 'Bryony Lester. Interior designer. Right?'

'R-right.'

'Diana tells me you're setting your cap straight at Jack Morgan?'

It was a blunt question, no holds barred. Bryony blinked back tears, took the proffered tea, and answered the question. It seemed totally stupid not to. Not when this woman could see her eyes, and Bryony's heart was in her eyes. She couldn't hide it.

'I love them both,' she whispered. 'Oh, dear God, is something really wrong?'

'It may be. I know Dr Hill's called in the consultant paediatrician and physician, so he's worried.' Then the nurse looked down at her for a long, long moment.

'Diana should have stayed,' she said irrelevantly.

Bryony didn't say a word.

'I'm not supposed to leave Casualty,' the nurse told Bryony at last. 'But heck...this is getting to me as well as you. Just answer the phone for me, do any resuscitation that comes your way, don't let any drunks throw up on my clean floor and I'll see if I can find out...'

And she left. Three minutes later Jack Morgan walked through the beige doors with the dragon lady following. Bryony's heart hit her boots.

If anything was needed to tell Bryony things were serious, Jack's face did. The man looked haggard, edge-of-a-nightmare haggard. He walked out blindly towards Bryony and stopped, and the dragon nurse followed him as though she feared he'd fall.

It was too much.

Bryony came to her feet. Her empty teacup clattered, unbreaking, to the floor and she took three running steps forward to take his hands, and hold him. The look in his eyes... She couldn't bear it.

'Jack...' Her voice was just plain terrified. 'Oh, Jack, what is it?'

'Bryony... How long have you been here?' he asked, and his voice was dazed.

'Three hours.' It was the dragon nurse answering for Bryony. Bryony couldn't. How could she possibly count hours? 'She's been here for three hours and she's looking near as bad as you. She needs to know.'

Jack closed his eyes—and his shoulders slumped. Bryony put her arms around him and held him hard. Not as a lover, just as one human being desperate to comfort another. 'Jack, was it something...was it the ride at the show? Has she torn something?' Bryony could hardly dare to ask.

But Jack shook his head. His face rested on her hair, as if he could find strength in touching her.

'No, Bryony. It's not your fault. It's no one's fault. The doctors say... They've tested her. She has bacterial meningitis.'

'Meningitis!'

Bryony rocked back on her heels, but her hands gripped Jack's convulsively. Meningitis. She knew it. A phantom disease that struck without warning. A child could be well one minute and dead within hours.

'Oh, Jack…'

There was dead silence while the enormity—the fear—washed over them both.

'How…how do they know?' she asked at last.

'They've done a lumbar puncture. They're sure now.'

'What…? Jack, what can they do?'

'They've loaded her with antibiotics. Blasted her… They started her on them even before the results of the tests came back. Because she got sick so fast, they suspected meningitis. But now… She's drifted into a coma.' Jack's voice cracked with strain. He shook his head as if to shake off the terror. 'Bryony, I have to get back.' Then he looked down at their linked hands. He should tell her to go home, to go to bed, as he'd told Diana to go.

He couldn't. Her hands were holding his, a fragile link to sanity.

'Stay,' he said, and Bryony nodded.

'I'll be right here if you need me. I'm going nowhere.'

'No.' He swallowed—a man right out of his depth. All he knew was that he needed her. He needed her right beside him.

'Stay with us,' he said, and he pulled her to the beige doors before she could argue. 'Stay with Maddy. Stay with me.'

It was the longest night of Bryony's life.

She sat in a corner of the intensive care unit while Jack sat at Maddy's bedside, and she prayed every prayer she'd ever been taught and a hundred more she thought up all by herself. She made promises and threats. Then she apologised for the threats and made promises again. She pleaded. She wept. But she didn't make a sound.

The doctors and nurses came and went—serious men and women in white coats with stethoscopes hanging round their necks and with faces as grave as death. There was a youngish man who seemed to be in charge, but there were more he called in—a specialist physician and a paediatrician and nurses…and heaven knew who they all were.

All Bryony knew was that they were fighting. They were fighting for something so precious she could hardly bear it. There was urgent talk of air ambulance transfers to Melbourne—but, by their quiet talk, Bryony knew the risks were too great for that. Please…

There was only room for Jack next to the bed. Jack sat, stony-faced, and held his daughter's unresponsive hand, but every now and then—as if desperate—his glance would swivel round to assure himself that Bryony was still there.

That he wasn't alone with his terror.

Please…

Maddy lay limply unconscious, as if she was slipping away already. Her face was deathly white on the pillows. The only colour was the incongruous old lion that Bryony had given her and Harry had chewed, lying beside her on the pillow.

Please…

Some time after dawn, or maybe it was closer to mid-morning—who'd know or even care?—Bryony's prayers were answered.

At first they weren't sure. The nurse took Maddy's temperature for the hundredth time—and frowned—and showed the doctor. He frowned and checked the charts, and then she took it again. She gave a tiny, frightened smile, as if she was afraid to hope.

Fifteen minutes later she took it again, and she and the doctor looked at each other and tried not to let optimism surge. Bryony could see it. There was hope—but they didn't want to raise Jack's hopes yet. To have to dash them again would be too cruel.

Then, suddenly, there was a flicker of an eyelid. That was all. It could almost have been imagined.

But the doctor was lifting Maddy's eyelids, checking her pupils with his torch, and then taking Maddy's hand from

Jack, and the hope that had been in his eyes was now in
his voice.

'Come on, Maddy. Come back to us.'

Nothing.

'I'm sure she's not slipping any deeper into coma,
though,' the doctor said. 'Her temperature's falling, and
that means the antibiotics are starting to work.' He glanced
at his watch. 'Twelve hours. It's possible.'

'But there might be damage…'

Jack didn't say any more, but Bryony knew what he
meant. Meningitis caused brain damage; she knew that.
Maddy didn't have to slip deeper. If she couldn't come
back to them…

She stared down at the still, frail body on the bed—and
the child's eyelid quivered again.

'Maddy…'

Bryony scarcely breathed the word. The whole world
held its breath. Jack sat immobile—a man afraid even to
admit the tiniest flicker of hope.

But she was sure she'd seen right. Bryony was unable to
stay in her corner now. She took three tentative steps to the
child's bed and grasped both Maddy's hands in hers. 'Come
on, sweetheart.' Bryony's voice firmed, strong and demanding. There mustn't be brain damage. No! 'Come on,
Maddy, love. Open your eyes. I'm here. Your daddy's here.
Open your eyes and see us.'

And Maddy did.

After that things sort of happened in a blur. Bryony howled
a lot. Jack held her and he held Maddy at the same time
and she thought he howled, too. Surely she was too wet
for her sogginess to be explained by one person's tears.

And Maddy smiled faintly—surely it was a smile!—and
drifted away from them again—but this time the doctor said
it was a natural sleep.

'We got it in time,' he said solemnly, but there was ju-
bilation beneath the fatigue in his voice. 'If we'd waited

until we knew…' He shook his head. 'She grew so sick so fast. Sometimes the only way is to go for broke with the antibiotics straight off.'

'Thank you, Doctor.' Jack wrung the doctor's hand and closed his eyes—and then he slumped back in the chair vacated by Bryony. When Bryony looked at the doctor who'd guided them through the night, there were tears in his eyes, too.

It was too much. Too much for Bryony. She needed to go and lock herself somewhere private and wail.

'I'll go, then…'

Jack looked up at that. 'No!'

It was a harsh outburst and it startled them all, but Maddy was asleep—and the dragon lady was peering around the door, her eyes asking a question.

'Is she okay? Sister Rodney says she's out of her coma and on the mend. Is it true? I can't go off duty until I know.'

The doctor's eyes said it all and the dragon lady came as close to a war dance as a middle-aged, starched ward sister could come. She smiled, she beamed, and she sighed. Then she passed on her messages.

'Diana Collins is out here asking to come in,' she said finally, and looked doubtfully across at Bryony. 'And Myrna Ferguson is in the waiting room asking for you, Miss Lester. She's been here for an hour now.'

Myrna…here… News must have travelled fast. This was a small farming community and news here sped like lightning. Everyone would be terrified by now—and the world was waiting to share their news. So Bryony managed a smile, albeit a watery one.

'They need to know. Myrna will be so frightened. And Harry's at home, Jack,' she said unsteadily. 'I have to tell him.'

She bent and kissed the sleeping child very gently on the forehead. Then, before Jack could stop her, she walked out and left him to his Diana.

* * *

There were more than two people in the waiting room when Bryony emerged. Jack had friends in the district—good friends—and they all wanted to help. The room was close to crowded.

Diana was first to greet her.

'What are *you* doing here?' she demanded, and Bryony gave her a watery smile. Not even Diana could spoil this morning.

'Maddy's going to make it,' she said shakily, and then turned to find Myrna at her side. 'Oh, Myrna...'

She looked helplessly at her friend. Before Diana could say a word, Myrna had whisked her right out of there and away from them all.

Myrna didn't say anything as she drove her home. It was only when she pulled up outside Bryony's cottage that Bryony realised her car was back at the hospital.

'Ian will bring it here later,' Myrna said roundly. 'You're not telling me you're fit to drive?'

'No. But...'

'Don't "but" me.' Myrna came around and opened the passenger door for her. 'Out. Shower. Breakfast. Bed. In that order.'

'I have appointments this morning,' Bryony said, in a voice that shook.

'Oh, yeah? You're going off to do them now, I suppose?' Myrna's voice was firm but kind. 'Bryony, pink fluffy slippers and eyes that match will not do this firm's reputation any good.'

Bryony stared down at her toes. Her slippers had been a farewell gift from a girlfriend in New York, and they looked like a cross between a feather boa and the Queen's best tiara.

They were something Bryony wore behind closed doors.

Bryony giggled, a trace of hysteria behind the laugh. 'Oh, heck. I've worn them all night.' Then her face crumpled. 'Oh, Myrna...'

'It's okay.' Myrna grabbed her friend and hugged her hard. 'It's okay, Bryony, love. Maddy's going to be okay.'

'Yes, she is,' Bryony wailed. 'But I love them both so much I can't bear it. What am I going to do?'

'I'll tell you what you're going to do,' Myrna said. 'You'll sleep for the rest of today, and then tonight you'll ring the hospital and find out if she's awake and then you'll go and see her. And you'll take it from there. One step at a time.'

'Diana doesn't want me there...'

'Hey, hang on.' Myrna held her friend at arm's length. 'Am I missing something here? Are we in love with Diana?'

'No. But...'

'Then let's get Diana out of the equation,' Myrna ordered. 'Right now.'

Only of course she couldn't.

Bryony went into the hospital that night to find Diana fielding Maddy's visitors. Jack was fast asleep in the next-door ward, and Diana told Bryony that, frankly, she wasn't wanted.

'No doubt you salved your conscience by staying up all night,' Diana told her. 'But you're not needed now. Madelaine's asleep and I told Jack I'd sit with her while he sleeps himself. But even if she wasn't asleep...'

Bryony got the point. Even if she wasn't asleep, Diana was the third point in their solid triangle. Bryony was the outsider.

She went home.

The next morning she rang before visiting hours, and, gloriously, she was put straight through to Maddy. There was a phone by her bed.

'Bryony!' Maddy's voice was weak but joyful on the other end of the line. 'Do you want to talk to Daddy? He's just gone to get me some lemonade but he'll be back here any minute.'

I'll just bet he will be, Bryony thought. Jack Morgan had come close to losing the most precious thing he had in the world and he wouldn't leave her now.

Jack...

Bryony tried to block out the thought of Jack Morgan by his little daughter's bedside, Jack with his face haggard with impending loss, Jack in her arms, Jack's look of tremulous joy when he knew Maddy would live. Jack saying, 'Stay.'

Stop it, Bryony, she told herself savagely. It was Maddy she was interested in. Only Maddy.

'Maddy, I don't need to talk to your daddy. I just want to talk to you. Can I come and visit?'

'Yes, please.' Maddy's voice was so definite it gave Bryony the courage she needed to slug Diana if she got in her way this time.

'Is there anything you want? Anything I can bring you?'

'Bring Harry,' Maddy said firmly. 'Daddy won't bring Jess in because she's so pregnant Daddy says she might have pups right on my bed.'

'Well, what's a hospital for? I thought lots of ladies had babies in hospital.'

'That's what I think but Daddy still won't bring her, and I really want to see Harry,' Maddy said in her yearning voice.

'Sweetheart, I don't know whether hospitals let dogs in...'

'Will you try?'

Good grief. But there was only one answer possible here.

'Yes.'

'Promise?'

'I promise to try.' Bryony grinned—and went to fetch her biggest coat.

The dragon lady was on the door. Bryony hiked up to the reception desk and greeted her as an old friend.

'How's Maddy?'

The nurse's eyes dropped to Bryony's midriff and stayed there—fascinated.

'She's fine.' The woman managed a vague smile, eyes still on Bryony's waist. 'Improving by leaps and bounds. She should be well enough to go home by the weekend.'

'That's great.' Bryony squared her shoulders and hoisted her tummy. 'Can I see her?'

The dragon lady pursed her lips and eyed the tummy with caution.

'I didn't realise you were pregnant, Miss Lester.'

'Oh, I'm not.' Bryony managed a cautious smile and fixed Dragon Lady with a look that was pleading as well as hopeful. 'I just drink too much beer. Can I see her now?'

Silence. Bryony's tummy wriggled.

'I think you'd better,' the dragon lady said, fascinated. 'Before...before your stomach gets away on you.'

Maddy had no visitors but Jack, and they were playing Scrabble. Maddy looked up from her game and squealed in delight as Bryony came through the door, and in two seconds Harry was squirming in her arms.

'Oh, you brought him. Oh, Harry...'

Jack was rising to his feet, and there was a look on his face that Bryony had never seen before. He hardly appeared to notice Harry.

'Bryony.'

It was a word. Just her name. But the way he said it sent goose bumps up and down her spine. She looked up at him—and the goose bumps grew goose bumps. He was looking at her as if...as if she was almost as precious as Maddy. She must be imagining it. A night without sleep could do strange things to a person.

Her night without sleep was twenty-four hours ago. And she'd slept since then. She flashed a rather frightened smile at him and crossed to hug his daughter.

'You look great, Maddy Morgan. They say it wasn't the

Tunnel of Doom that caused it, though I have my doubts myself.'

'It wasn't,' Maddy said indignantly. 'Diana just says it was because she doesn't like you.'

'Well, Harry doesn't approve of the Tunnel of Doom either,' Bryony said solidly, turning the subject adroitly from Diana and ignoring the strange look in Jack's eyes. Or almost ignoring the strange look in Jack's eyes. 'Harry's a very sensible dog. He stayed really still when we came in here.'

'People saw you...' Jack was fascinated.

'Yep. I thought I might get grabbed on the way and re-routed to Maternity, but I made it through.' She looked doubtfully at the door. 'But this had better be a flying visit, Maddy, love. If someone comes...'

'No one will,' Maddy said definitely, and took Harry under her bedclothes for a private chat. Bryony was left looking at Jack.

'Thank you for being here the other night,' he said slowly, and his look didn't change. 'I needed you.'

Boy. *There* was an admission. It took Bryony's breath right away. I needed you, too, she felt like saying—but she didn't. She'd thrown herself at this man one time too many.

It was over to him now; he could take her or leave her. The only problem was, if he left her she'd break her heart.

'Maddy's coming home on Friday,' he said. 'Will you come to dinner on Saturday?'

'I'd love to.'

This was a start. This was definitely hopeful. But Maddy was peering out over her bedcover, frowning.

'I thought Diana said she was cooking our dinners at the weekend.'

'Did she?' Jack said blankly. 'I don't...' He put a hand to his head and Bryony saw that he was still sleep-deprived. He was still in a haze where he hadn't realised Maddy was fully restored to him. He'd come awfully close to a precipice and it was taking him time to accept his feet were on solid earth again. Maybe when he did he wouldn't want her to come to dinner.

'Leave it,' she said gently. 'Get yourselves back home and settled and then think about it.'

Her voice was firmer than she felt herself.

'I don't...'

Jack didn't get any further.

The door swung open, and it was Diana.

'You!'

For a fleeting moment Bryony felt it in her to be sorry for the girl. Diana must be in love herself to react to Bryony with this amount of hate. Her voice was pure vitriol.

And then she saw Harry.

'You've brought your dog!' Her voice was practically a screech. 'Of all the stupid, crass things... You bring a dog in here? Don't you realise how close this child came to death? The last thing she needs now is dogs—covered in germs—and in her bed, for heaven's sake...'

She stepped forward, grabbed Harry by the collar and fair hurled him out of the door. Harry landed with a sickening thud out in the corridor, and he cringed. There were echoes in Harry's memory, echoes of raised voices and kicks, echoes of pain. Months of living with Bryony had made the echoes fade but they were still there. He knew what anger meant.

So he shoved his stumpy tail between his leg and scuttled down the shiny corridor as fast as his little legs would scuttle.

'No!'

'Diana...'

'Harry!'

The three voices rose in simultaneous protest, but before Diana could say one more word—before anyone could—Bryony dived out of the door and was off after her beloved dog. He was going fast. As Bryony hit the corridor, she saw a flash of stumpy tail heading west around a corner.

When she hit the corner she saw him flying through an open door—a door labelled 'Nursing Home'.

Then through another small corridor and another door...

Bryony burst through the door, out of breath, to find three old ladies staring with bright-eyed interest. Two ladies were in armchairs watching television. A third old lady—tiny and wizened with age—was a frail bump in a corner bed.

'Did you see a dog?' Bryony managed, hanging onto the door and fighting for breath. 'A little grey dog...'

'Who, us?' one of the ladies watching television demanded. She fiddled with the remote control of the television, ostensibly to turn down the volume but in reality to get her face in order. Then she gazed up at Bryony with limpid and innocent eyes.

Despite her worry, Bryony had to smile. As a con man, this lady left a lot to be desired. Hmm. She looked all around the room. So where was he?

'Do you mind if I just check? He might have come in while you were watching television.'

'You check, dear.' Three pairs of eyes were watching her, with various degrees of speculation, and a certain amount of judgement. Harry had looked terrified.

'Harry?'

Nothing.

Short of searching drawers and wardrobes, there was nothing for it. Bryony fixed the would-be con lady with a look of determination.

'His name's Harry,' she said. ''He's scared. He's been hurt and he's mine. I love him.'

Silence, while the three old ladies took that on board, and checked Bryony out from the toes up. Finally—results. Until now, the old lady on the bed hadn't moved. Now, though, a gnarled old arm raised itself from the bedclothes. It dropped downwards, and a bent old finger pointed straight under the bed beneath her. Bryony stared, and then she stooped. Way back in the corner, huddled in the dark, two little eyes stared out in terror.

It was too much.

Bryony was under there in a flash, crawling right under, hauling Harry into her arms, holding him close, and there she stayed, tucked in the safety of the darkness with her dog.

'Oh, Harry... Oh, Harry, she hurt you...'

He was shaking like a leaf.

She put her face in his fur and felt like bursting into tears. There were two of them here—she and Harry—and both of them were suffering various degrees of emotional trauma. They were in this together. Then Bryony froze as she heard heavy footsteps down the corridor, and someone at the door. A voice...

'Has anyone here seen a dog? And his owner? A girl with bright red hair...'

Jack. It was Jack. Silence.

Bryony's heart missed several beats.

'Who, us?' the same old lady said again.

There was silence again as Jack thought about it, but finally he came to the same conclusion Bryony had.

'The dog's scared,' he said finally—gently. 'Someone hurt him. I swear it wasn't me. I couldn't hurt him. And the lady he's with...I need to find her. You see, I love her. I love them both.'

More silence. Dead silence. Bryony held her breath. Harry held his breath, too. And then, up above her, the gnarled old arm was raised again from the bedclothes—and once again it pointed straight down.

Straight down to where the fugitives were hiding.

Jack stared. Then, bemused, he crossed the room to look for himself.

'Bryony?'

He bent to peer under the bed. He could hardly see her, but he could see enough. Bryony's eyes were filled with uncertainty, and Harry's eyes were still filled with fear.

Two seconds later, Jack Morgan was under the bed, holding Bryony and Harry together in his arms in the darkness as if he'd never let them go.

When they finally surfaced it was to let Bryony sneeze.

To kiss and sneeze at the same time was difficult—but not impossible. Bryony was on her third sneeze before Jack eased his hold. Even then it was with reluctance—and he let her go a whole two inches.

'There are fluff balls under this bed,' Bryony managed shakily, her sneezes muffled by Jack's chest. 'I think we need to report the cleaners for shoddy work here.'

'Let's not,' Jack said into her hair, and pulled her close again. 'I think fluff balls are great.'

That had about three meanings. Bryony considered, and decided she liked them all.

'Don't whinge,' a voice above them ordered. The voice was cracked with age, querulous but still laced with humour. 'I don't let 'em vacuum under my bed more'n once a week. It makes me nervous.'

'Do we make you nervous?' Jack asked, grinning into Bryony's hair. His arms were holding her tight against him. There was hardly enough room for the three of them under the bed—but there was enough.

'Who, me?' the voice said. 'Nah. I like company. If you get too much for me I'll shove a knitting needle down between the springs.'

Bryony choked—and Jack's grin broadened and he went straight back to kissing her again.

They didn't surface for quite some time. Bryony figured she didn't want to surface ever. Her hands were holding Jack against her and she was feeling as if there were miracles all around her here, everywhere.

They had an audience, she knew. There was no sound from above, the three ladies waiting with courteous patience for their guests to emerge.

Harry's shivering had stopped. He was squashed some-

where between man and woman, and the faint stirring of
his stumpy backside told them he was quite happy with the
way things were turning out here.

'Jack...'

'Mmm?' He let her go for a fraction of a second and
somehow she got his name out. Then he kissed her again.

'Did I hear you right?' she whispered at last. 'Did you
say you loved me?'

'He did!' The ancient voice cackled from above them,
and the bed springs bounced so close, both Bryony and Jack
had to slide down further. 'I heard him.'

'We did, too.' The two other ladies spoke in unison. The
television had been turned right off. They had much better
entertainment right under the bed. 'He can't get out of it
now.'

'I don't want to,' Jack said firmly, and he kissed her yet
again. His kiss this time was so long and so possessive and
so thorough that he took her breath completely away. It
didn't matter. What did she need to breathe for, after all?

The darkness and fluff and the fact that they were sitting
under an old lady's bed in a nursing home misted away
into nothing at all. There was only each other. There was
only their love. There was only this kiss.

It couldn't last for ever.

Finally there were voices from above. It was Diana, and
someone else, someone echoing starch.

Diana's voice sounded first. The venom was still there.
'I tell you, she brought a dog into the hospital. She has to
be somewhere round here with her stupid mutt.'

'Well, if we find her we'll ask her to leave, but that's all
we can do.' It was Starch. 'Have any of you ladies seen a
woman with a dog?'

'Who, us?'

Same response. Bryony cringed against Jack, waiting for
Diana and Starch to haul her out of here and out of Jack's
arms. But this time it was different. This time it was the

lady on the bed speaking, and her ancient voice held incredulity that anything so out of the way could happen.

'No, Matron, there's been no one come in all morning. Oh, Miss Collins... I remember you. How are you? How's your mother and father? And your great-aunty Maud? Your aunty and I were friends when we were girls. Let's see now, what are all her grandchildren up to? Come and sit here and tell me all about them. Gerard must be your age. And Louise and Marianne and Peter and Sam...'

Diana couldn't get away fast enough. Diana and Starch retreated.

Bryony choked into her lover's arms.

'Marry me,' Jack demanded, and the whole world stopped.

Bryony froze.

'What...what did you say?'

'He said marry him,' the voice above them boomed. The occupant of the top floor was shedding weakness by the minute. 'It's us who are supposed to be deaf, not you.'

'He doesn't mean it,' Bryony managed. Jack was holding her close in the dark and she could feel the beat of his heart against her breast.

'I do mean it,' Jack said strongly. 'I've never meant anything so much in my life before.'

'Don't matter if he doesn't,' the voice operating the bed springs said. 'Accept first, ask questions later. Jack Morgan's okay, girl. His grandpa was okay, too. Thought about marrying him myself!'

Bryony choked again, but when her laughter died she knew what she had to say.

'Jack, no.'

Jack cupped her chin in his hand and looked fair square into her eyes in the dim light. 'What do you mean—no? You have to marry me. You must. Bryony Lester, I love you.'

'But...you love me against your better judgement.'

'That's not true.'

'You think Diana would be a more sensible wife.'

'I don't.'

'Of course he doesn't.' The voice again. 'The man'd be a fool to want that cold fish...'

'Jack, you're exhausted and distraught...'

'I'm only distraught when I look at you...'

'You need sleep...'

'You want me to vacate the bed?' The old lady above them was having the time of her life. The bed springs were definitely bouncing. But it was all just too much, overwhelmingly too much. Bryony hauled herself out from under, with Harry nestled securely in her arms, and she looked down as Jack emerged after her.

There was fluff on his eyebrows. Dear heaven, she loved him more than life itself, and because she loved him she knew what she had to say.

'Jack, I won't be proposed to like this,' she whispered. 'Not when you're exhausted and emotional and not...not thinking straight.'

He stood looking directly into her eyes, *his* eyes loving her.

'I'm thinking straighter now than I have for years,' he told her. His voice was deep and steady and sure, filled with love.

'No.' She took a deep breath. He'd wake up tomorrow and be appalled at what he'd done. Trapped. 'No one proposes sensibly under beds in nursing homes.'

'Yes, they do,' the bed-bound lady cackled. 'He just did. We heard him. You have three witnesses, girl. He can't get out of this one.'

'He can.' Bryony took another deep breath. Because she loved him so much, he could.

'Jack, you married Georgia and you made a mistake,' she managed. 'I won't let you rush in and marry me against your better judgement. No matter how much I love you. I'm not saying I won't marry you. But I...I won't take this seriously unless you think about it for a bit. So...so you get some sleep. Take Maddy home. Think about it clearly. And...and if you still want to marry me then—'

She broke off and Jack took a step towards her. She put Harry up before her to fend him off.

'No!' She backed away from him. 'It's nearly killing me to say this, Jack Morgan, but I won't marry you unless you think...unless you think it's sensible!'

'You told him *what*?'

Myrna paced.

'Bryony, are you out of your mind? This time you have finally flipped. *Unless he thinks it's sensible.* What sort of ultimatum is that? This is the most goose-brained, illogical, twit-haired scheme...'

'It's what I have to do,' Bryony said sadly.

'But...why?'

'Because I love him.'

There was nothing more to say.

CHAPTER TWELVE

MADDY rang on Friday night, just after sunset. Not Jack. Maddy.

Bryony launched herself at the phone on the first ring. She'd been doing it for two days now and there were grooves dug in the wall where she'd landed too fast and knocked the phone into the plaster.

For two days it hadn't been Jack, and now it was Maddy.

'Bryony, you have to come.'

It was a breathless whisper and it brought Bryony up short.

'What's wrong? Maddy, are you okay?'

'Daddy brought me home from hospital this afternoon and I'm fine. But now we think Jessica's having her puppies. Daddy's with her and he says you have to come fast—and I think you should bring Harry.'

It was just as well there were no speed cameras between Bryony's cottage and the farm because she would have been a sitting duck for some hefty fines. She had managed to take off her crazy slippers and don some respectable sneakers with her jeans and sweater before she'd left, but it was a tousled and breathless Bryony who knocked on the farm door fifteen minutes later.

Jack opened the door. The urgency faded. Bryony stood on the doorstep and couldn't remember why she'd come.

'Bryony…'

'Jack…'

She took a deep breath and tried to think. Harry wriggled from her arms and shot into the house, and Jack snapped out of his trance.

'You brought the dog,' he said, stunned—and then he swore and the spell was completely broken. 'Hell, Bryony, Jessie's in labour. Bitches in labour won't let dogs near them...'

And he took off after Harry.

Here we go again... Bryony closed her eyes. Maddy had said to bring Harry, so she had. She hadn't thought...

'The whole trouble with you, Bryony Lester, is that you don't think,' she told herself savagely, and followed Jack and Harry towards the living room.

She stopped in the doorway. So did Jack. Jack had been afraid that Jess would object violently to Harry's presence, but the scene that met their eyes was one of pure harmony.

There was a fire burning in the grate. The overhead light was off and, apart from the flickering of flames, there was no light apart from a weak lamp set by the dog's basket. Jessica was waiting quietly in her basket by the fireside for her pups to come.

Maddy was lying on the sofa. The little girl was swathed in blankets and fast asleep.

Harry had bounded right up to Jessica. Now Jess was standing up in her basket, her body swollen with pups. There was no fear and no aggressive reaction at all as Harry arrived. Jessica greeted her love with quiet dignity, nose to nose, and then she slumped her heavy body down into her basket again.

Then, while they watched in awe, Harry put his nose on his paws and settled as well, right beside the basket. No matter that Bryony had just brought him into a strange house full of exciting new smells; Harry was where he wanted to be.

'Well, how about that?' Jack's arm came around Bryony's waist and held tight. 'A man who knows where he belongs.'

'I'm...I'm sorry.' It was hard to make her voice work when Jack's arm was linking his body to hers. 'I shouldn't have brought him. Maddy told me to bring him when she phoned.'

Then she had another dreadful thought. Had Maddy phoned because Jack wanted her? Or because Maddy wanted her?

'You did want me to come?' Bryony asked, in a small voice.

'Of course we did.' There was no doubting the strength or conviction of Jack's reply.

In fact, he'd been counting the hours until he could get her here. He'd planned this time. He'd wanted an evening, a whole evening. The times between visiting Maddy in hospital weren't enough, but now Maddy was home.

'Maddy and I talked about it,' he told her, his eyes devouring her. 'We were planning to wait until tomorrow and put on a special dinner for you, to say everything we wanted to say, but when Jess went into labour...' He paused and smiled then, his own heart-warming smile that had Bryony's heart doing handstands.

'I thought the pups might come fast. I set up the basket by the fire so Maddy could watch, and while I was doing that Maddy phoned you. She must have decided for herself that Harry had to come.'

'But...' Bryony looked around the room, trying to focus on something that wasn't Jack. 'Maddy's asleep.'

'Maddy's exhausted. She's only been home for two hours. She tried to stay awake until you came but she couldn't. I promised I'd wake her as soon as the pups started arriving.'

'But...the pups...' She frowned. 'Shouldn't she be having them? There's not one stuck or something dreadful, is there?'

'No. Jess would be more distressed if that was happening. She just seems to have gone off the boil for a bit.'

'Oh.' Bryony nodded knowledgeably. 'That's medical terminology, is it?' she asked. '"Gone off the boil"?'

'Yep.' He grinned and there was sheer happiness blazing

in his eyes. 'Absolutely. Ranks right up there with big words like haemophilia and osteoporosis. See? I'm trained for anything.'

Bryony chuckled.

Jack looked at the girl before him, and his heart was exposed for all to see.

Silence.

Harry was washing his paws, quietly content. Jessica was snoozing. The fire was crackling in the grate. And Bryony and Jack stood facing each other in the firelight, with Bryony wondering where to start.

'I thought... It was really hard to get her voice to work. 'I thought Diana would be here tonight.'

'No.'

'Why not?'

'Diana hit Harry,' Jack said softly, his eyes still smiling. 'Some things are unforgivable. Bryony, Diana has been my neighbour for all my life. For a while I wondered if she could be more than that. I was mad.'

'Jack...'

'Bryony, I've been thinking,' he told her, placing a finger on her lips to silence her. 'Let me finish. Let me say what I need to.' He reached down and took her hands in his, strongly, surely. 'I've been thinking about what you said, about me marrying you against my better judgement. It's not true.'

'It is.' Bryony swallowed. 'It must be.'

'No. Bryony, I tried to convince myself to marry Diana. I tried to convince myself it was sensible. If I'd been stupid enough to succeed then that would have been marrying someone against my better judgement.'

Things had changed. *Things had changed!* Bryony looked wonderingly up at her love, hardly daring to breathe. Please...

Jack sighed, and his hold on her hands tightened. 'Bryony, it's true I've made mistakes in the past. I married Georgia and that was a disaster. But...it wasn't a disaster because I didn't love her. It was a disaster for different reasons, for reasons outside the marriage. It was a disaster because Georgia hadn't achieved her dream and her dream wasn't here, so she changed. She let her unhappiness eat at her and it killed what chance of happiness we had; it killed our love.

'But at least we had that chance to begin with,' he added softly. 'Diana and I don't have that chance. We don't love each other; we never have. Whereas you and I...'

You and I...

There was a nightingale singing outside somewhere, Bryony thought irrelevantly. She'd never heard a nightingale in her life before, and they surely didn't exist in this country, but she was hearing nightingales now.

'You and I...?' It was all she could do to get the whisper past her lips.

'Bryony, you've said you love me.' Jack closed his eyes as though he was afraid that something of infinite value was about to be taken away from him. 'Bryony... Is that still true?'

'Yes.'

That was all she said; it was all she could say. Nothing more. One simple word that echoed around and around the room. And Jack opened his eyes and there was a joy in his look that blazed like the firelight it reflected.

'Truly?'

'Truly, Jack,' Bryony whispered. 'I loved you the first time I saw you and I've loved you ever since. All the time without stopping, now and for ever, whether you want me or whether you don't.'

'Dear God.' It was a prayer, a benediction of thankfulness.

'I loved you, too,' Jack said then, and he pulled her roughly into his arms. 'Beloved Bryony. With your crazy, lovely ways of meeting the world head-on, of running through life with joy. I loved you, but I was afraid to show it, afraid of what I felt. Bryony, I want you... I want you so much I ache at night for you. I ache...I ache all the time...'

Bryony let herself fall against his chest, her body pressing full length against his. Joy was running through her in lovely slivers of light. She pressed harder and she knew what he said was true.

She placed her hands up on his jaw and cupped his face—and stood on tiptoes to kiss his mouth. Then she was being gathered to him in a sweeping gesture of love and possession and pride. And triumph. She was being spun around the room, laughing and crying in his arms—light and high and filled with a pure, blasting happiness.

The kiss was deepening, the whirling stopped. They were sinking down onto the carpet.

'This carpet's not soft enough,' Jack growled. 'Can we bring your rugs here? All of them?'

'All...?'

'All.'

'I'll think about it,' she promised, kissing him tenderly on the face and then moving so her lips were on the bare skin exposed by his open shirt. 'I'll think of anything you like. Tomorrow...'

And her hands moved under his shirt.

'Bryony...'

'Mmm?'

His voice was husky with desire, with urgency. 'Bryony, did you bring your condom supply?'

That stopped her. She sat up as if she'd been shot. Boy, she could enjoy rubbing this one in!

'Are you kidding, Jack Morgan? I'm not engaged to be married any more. So I don't carry condoms. I flushed the whole lot.'

'You flushed...'

'It was the only respectable thing to do,' she explained, only a dimple at the side of her mouth giving her inward laughter, her inner joy, away. 'And I'll have you know I'm always respectable.'

'But you're respectably engaged to be married.'

'Am I?' She was rolling underneath him, running her hands through his hair, loving him, devouring him.

'You are. You definitely are. Four weeks, Ian said. Four weeks is the legal minimum, before we can be properly married.'

'I haven't said yes yet.'

He hauled her sweater up and kissed each nipple in turn. He teased. He taunted, and then rolled her over so she was underneath. He pushed himself up so he was laughing down at her.

'Say yes.'

'Yes.'

'Bryony…'

The laughter died. There was only love. And then there was a faint whimper—and Jack and Bryony rolled as one to see what was happening by the fire.

Jessica's body was heaving in the firelight.

Jack turned up the floor lamp and Bryony rolled closer to see, and to stay by her love, for ever. Harry was standing by the basket, peering down, looking worried.

Another whimper.

Jack looked closely down into the basket—and he smiled. He kissed Bryony on the nose, disengaged their tangled limbs, and then rose and lifted his little daughter off the couch. Maddy half woke, lying in his arms and looking up at her father with dazed and sleepy wonder.

'Harry junior's just been born,' he told her. 'Watch. This one might be Harriet.'

It was. They watched with awe as five tiny grey and black and white puppies slipped effortlessly into the world—a crazy, beautiful mix of Jessie and Harry. Wonderful, unique puppies. Puppies that would sell to good homes in a flash—if ever they could bear to part with them.

Not all of them, Bryony thought dizzily. Maddy needed one of her own and maybe one could be a wedding present just for her…

They were truly gorgeous puppies. It was a truly gorgeous night. It was a night of miracles.

And Harry sat beside the basket and beamed with what Bryony could have sworn was paternal pride.

'Harry really loves Jessica,' Bryony said softly, rubbing his muzzle. 'He really does.'

'Of course he does,' Maddy said sleepily as her father tucked her back on her couch. 'Harry loves Jessica. Everyone knows that.'

'And I love you,' Jack told his daughter, kissing her gently. 'And Maddy...I love Bryony, too. We could be a family. Would you like that?'

'Yes, I would.' Maddy was so close to sleep that her words were a faint blur. 'Of course I would. Harry loves Jessica. Daddy loves Bryony. I love Bryony...'

Bryony closed her eyes and thought life couldn't get much better than this.

'And I love you all,' she whispered.

Then Jack gathered her into his arms. How could she have thought life couldn't get much better than this?

It did.

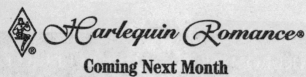

Coming Next Month

#3559 THE ONE-WEEK MARRIAGE Renee Roszel
Isabel has always played down her looks around her boss. But now he
wants her to pretend to be his "wife" for a week, and she knows, as she
sheds her drab feathers, Gabe will be in for the shock of his life!

#3560 TO TAME A BRIDE Susan Fox
Maddie St. John is everything Lincoln Coryell despises in a woman—
she's glamorous, socially privileged and devotes all her time to looking
good! Linc has to admit she's certainly gorgeous. But when they're
stranded alone together, he discovers that Maddie isn't just a spoiled
socialite. She has a loving heart—and Linc could be the man to tame
her!

Rebel Brides: *Two rebellious cousins—and the men who tame them!*

#3561 FARELLI'S WIFE Lucy Gordon
When Franco Farelli had married Joanne's cousin, Joanne had
graciously stepped aside, her love for Franco kept secret. Now he was
begging her to stay, if only for his motherless son's sake. But Joanne
needed to believe his desire for her wasn't because she resembled her
cousin, but because he wanted her for herself....

Kids & Kisses: *Where kids and kisses go hand in hand!*

#3562 BACHELOR COWBOY Patricia Knoll
Luke had been an infuriating puzzle to Shannon since their first
prickly meeting. Now he was desperate for her help, having been left in
charge of his baby nephew. As she taught him how to take care of little
Cody, Shannon saw that Luke's defenses were melting—just like her
heart....

Marriage Ties: *The four Kelleher women, bound together by family
and love.*